SLIP OF THE TONGUE
& OTHER STORIES

SLIP OF THE TONGUE
& OTHER STORIES
JOHNNY STANTON

TOUGH POETS PRESS
ARLINGTON, MASSACHUSETTS

Copyright © 1968, 1969, 1970, 1971, 1973, 1978, 2024 by Johnny Stanton.

Some of these works first appeared in *Adventures in Poetry, The Columbia Review, Sun, Telephone,* and *The World.* "Slip of the Tongue" was originally published by Angel Hair Books in 1969. "The Day Our Turtle Was Kidnapped" was originally published by Siamese Banana Press in 1978.

All rights reserved.

Back cover photo by Anthony J. Morenzi.

ISBN 979-8-218-45548-4

Tough Poets Press
Arlington, Massachusetts 02476
U.S.A.

www.toughpoets.com

For Sean and Sam,
my two terrific sons

CONTENTS

Goin' to Work, Lewis 9
The Most Unforgettable Character I Ever Met 12
In the Moonlight 15
From The Jissom Trail .16
Why I Like to Write?! 35
First Completed Pass of the Day 36
From Helping the Guy with the Prostitutes 38
Somebody's Always Winning 46
Mother of God 56
Modern Love 65
Saturday (el Sábado) 88
Tales of Sean and Sam 90
The Day Our Turtle Was Kidnapped 92
Open Postcard Story .106
Slip of the Tongue 107

About the Author 135
Acknowledgments 137

GOIN' TO WORK, LEWIS

Heard tell that there's been much critic shit spew about friendly lower east side poets putting their everyday, day after day, joy, sorrow, and energies into their poems.

Goddammit! Imagine writing a poem about getting up in the refreshing haze of morning, smoking dope, eating pussy, running up and down exciting black white puerto rican streets, yelling with sheer rage and eagerness, shooting your old lady, your flesh everyday falling on the ground crazy in the upheaval of joyfire, you keeping your hands hot on the hidden pulse of things, and you striding leaping flying across the inner dawn of life....

Man, the way I got it figured out, if poets put their everyday life into their work, I oughta write a work about my everyday life.

I work at a restaurant every day, Monday thru Friday, in the 42nd Street business district, taking outgoing food orders from 11 to 3 on the telephone....

"Hello, Fountain."
"I'd like to make an outgoing order, please."
"To where?"
"67 West 44th St.... Room 901." (I write this down on an order blank.)

"Ma'am, do I need an individual name or extension in there?"

"Well, my name is Sheila, and my extension is 326."

"Thank you, ma'am. Your order, please."

"First, I'd like a roast beef, rare, on whole wheat bread." (I write this down.)

"Do you want butter and lettuce on that sandwich, ma'am?"

"Oh... I'll have some lettuce and a little mayonnaise, please." (I write this down.)

"No butter, ma'am?"

"No. No butter." (I write this down.)

"Yes, ma'am."

"Also I want a tunafish salad on rye toast, high and dry, hold everything." (I write this down.)

"Yes, ma'am."

"And a hot corn beef on rye." (I write this down.)

"Yes, ma'am."

"And I'd like a banana on a roll." (I write this down.)

"Butter and lettuce on that, ma'am?"

"No, I don't think so."

"Yes, ma'am."

"Do you have any fresh fruit salad?"

"Yes, ma'am."

"I want three of them." (I write this down.) "And what's your soup of the day?"

"Yankee bean and chicken noodle, ma'am."

"Never mind about the soup."

"Yes, ma'am. Do you want anything to drink?"

"Yes. Two regular coffees, a diet cola, a lite coffee, and a cherry coke."

"That's two regulars, one lite, a diet cola, and a cherry coke, ma'am."

"Yes, that's right."

"Is there anything else, ma'am?"

"No, I think that's it."

"Yes, ma'am."
"Oh, don't forget to put in some extra pickles."
"Yes ma'am. That's room 901, in 67, extension 326."
"Yes, that's correct."
"Thank you, ma'am."
"Goodbye."
"So long, sweetheart."

THE MOST UNFORGETTABLE CHARACTER I EVER MET

It's noon. I'm working on my job. Newsstand, 42nd Street and 5th Avenue. Joe, the telegram routeman's helper, struts up to the stand. He smiles widely and says, "Hi Johnny, what do you say?"

"Nothing much, Joe. Business is a little slow."

He shrugs his shoulders, blows his nose with his fingers, coughs, and spits on the sidewalk. He yawns. The top of Joe's upper teeth are very green, almost black. Joe is an ex-criminal. He's stocky, greasy, and almost bald. He has pop-eyes. Joe likes to tell me about the business he was in. When he was sixteen, he robbed his father's best friend as he, the friend, was coming down the stairs of Joe's house. Joe's father was strong, mustachioed, olive-faced, masculine, no-speaka-the-english Italian immigrant.

When Joe was seventeen, he and some friends would drive around Harlem looking for floating crap games. If they saw a crap game, they would scream, "Here comes the cops!" The men playing craps would run, leaving all their money. Joe and his friends would jump out, take the money, and then take off in their car.

Joe did almost nine years in the state penitentiary. He had robbed sixty-four houses before he was caught. The last house he robbed was a judge's on Long Island. He gun-whipped the judge and smacked the judge's wife. His record was so bad the army wouldn't take him to fight in World War II.

I told Joe I was arrested in Houston, Texas, for robbing a Weingarten supermarket. I mentioned how well protected the store was with an eight-man private guard agency toting shotguns. I spent a month in Houston County Jail. When my trial came up I was sentenced to thirty days after pleading guilty to my robbery and a few others. Joe knew what a cop-out court was.

Now Joe is married and has four kids. His wife is expecting another in September. One of Joe's daughters is an epileptic. She is eleven years old. Joe says the doctor said that Joe's daughter's seizures will lessen and eventually disappear as the girl has her period.

Joe's wife had a nervous breakdown six years after they were married. For two years Joe had to watch her very carefully because she wanted to kill their kids at night. Also, she didn't want to have intercourse and she walked in her sleep. Her doctor said she was worrying too much about her sick mother. Her brothers and sisters always gave her a hard time about Mother and how sick Mother was. Joe's wife is now cured but when Joe's wife gets smart, he jokingly says that if she doesn't stop he'll put her in the crazy house.

Joe's wife told him about her girlfriend, Mrs. X. Mrs. X's husband was playing around with Mrs. X's sister. Mrs. X knew about it and told him to stop. He denied everything. Mrs. X went to see her sister. Her sister denied everything. She said, "Don't blame me if you can't keep your husband." One night, Mrs. X's husband went out after dinner to go to the neighborhood bar. When he left, Mrs. X called Mr. Y, her sister's husband and told him to come over immediately. When Mr. Y arrived, Mrs. X made him comfortable on the sofa. She gave him a drink and went into the bedroom. She reappeared naked. Mr. Y became red and tried to leave but Mrs. X grabbed him by the penis and brought him back into the bedroom. Afterwards, Mrs. X called her sister while Mr. Y was sitting beside her. Mrs. X said that she had just made love to Mr. Y and she knew that her husband was there with her sister. She told her sister to come over and get Mr. Y and bring back Mr. X. That's all

Joe told me.

Joe smokes three packs of menthol cigarettes a day. Sometimes he smokes four. At present, Joe and his family are on relief but the other day Joe was telling me he makes about $120 a week tax free. That includes the money his wife gets from the Welfare Department for support of the kids. Joe at one time or another was a house robber, counterfeiter, cabinet maker, license plate maker, longshoreman, tile worker, boilermaker, construction worker, numbers runner, policy man, maintenance man, bodyguard, night club bouncer, grocery clerk, lover, father, brother, son, husband, belt maker, wine drinker, young punk, cop hater, liberal, conservative, handyman, plumber, steel worker, and assistant telegram routeman.

Joe asked, "How's the kid, Johnny?" I say, "Well, he's a little sick. He has a cold." Joe says, "When my kids have a cold I take some thick orange peels and put them in boiling water. Let them boil for around ten minutes. When it cools, make the kid drink it. The oil the orange peels make is very good for the kids. It gives them resistance." While Joe is talking I nod my head approvingly. I say, "That sounds great, Joe. I'll try it on Sean tonight." Joe says, "It'll work. I know it'll work."

We don't talk for five minutes. Both of us look at girls going by. Sometimes Joe whistles or makes a remark. Then Joe says, "I'll see you later, Johnny. I'm going down the block to see my brother. I have to see him about something." I say, "Okay, I'll see you later, Joe."

IN THE MOONLIGHT

"I have a perfect horror of pianos," the old Jew said to me.

He lived in the suburbs and was a clerk in the Public Education Office. He took the bus to work every morning, sitting opposite a girl with whom he fell in love.

We were in a procession walking along a road which was shaded by tall oak trees.

"Come home with me," he said, "you handsome dark fellow. I'm very nice. Come on. You'll be able to warm yourself, I have a comfortable fire at home."

I had invested all my money in his lousy piano company. I had been hoping for a great success. I had even left my job at the theater. For more than a month now I've been looking everywhere for work.

The jew was busy with his own thoughts. He had the look of a man who was dreaming and trying to remember something. He said:

"I'm thinking about a slow yet passionate piece of music that I once heard. It was played by a woman with blond silky hair. Her hair was very beautiful. I wished that I could cut it off after she died, and twist it into a bow for my violin."

from
THE JISSOM TRAIL

On this Planet

Just in from radioactive desert galaxy first Bugger Gang wasted away most of their years on this planet searching for machine parts in heavy metal sea. It took them long time to give up hope, to settle down, to realize that they were going to stay here forever, or until the Rival Union collapses, and new representatives of free planet bipeds regain old knowledge of intergalactic leap, lost through filth, laziness, ignorance, and corruption.

But now, how could Bugger Gang ever know what was taking place in Red Terrestrial Galaxy? They had collected and brought with them all the important knowledge concerning big jump-off. They left behind only fragments of minor plan tapes, as mysterious clues, aware in full detail that powerful religion would be formed around these pieces. No one would fathom what secret details referred to.

Unfortunately Bugger Gang also lost their grip on total galactic jump-off. It was after they had come through to this planet—their sixth galaxy leap—to look see if they could plant a Colony here. Most of Bugger Gang went out in the landing party. There had been too many giddy festivities celebrating this breakthrough. Everyone was feeling lightheaded with the unbounding exuberance of infinite space. This planet looked good. They had landed on the shore of dark yellow sea. They thought they might be able to live here in sweet peace and freedom.

The people, who left to check on conditions of habitation, were working at great distance from huge galactic transport, which could house an earth city of seven thousand. Dark clouds approached and soft blue flames. Pale glimpses of shining metal and heavy blocks were hurtled through the air.

The next norning the ship was torn apart. . . .

Bewildering mystery mingled with horrors of death. . . .

Scattered rubble crisscrossed the sand, only small wooden boats were still intact. Everything else, including space communicators and jump-off memory banks, had vanished.

Bugger Gang went crazy, stayed that way for a good number of years, aimlessly searching, mostly on the sea, for parts of their lost space ship.

They should have explored more land. . . .

Their future generations could only bite into narrow strip of land: interior of the continent was protected from pounding on ocean. . . .

Flesh seekers and panic dwarfs came out of the ground. They licked their greasy fingers. There were several desperate fights in the moonless black darkness of night. Bugger Gang inflated their own skins and switched on lights in their hands. They won, but were forced to hack off their recently acquired clutching feelers. . . .

The evolution of Bugger Gang from rigid body to flexible body was accomplished in only four life durations, then fashion for new and peculiar body formations became their dominant principle. Nevertheless a few structures became permanent: no eyelids, a bow and arrow chest, yellow skin with patches of green, no ears—just four pinpricks, where sensitive, well-protected audio brain tubes pick up every kind of sound within distance of half mile—and during the last two decades it was decided that bone formation of circular feet, from double boat ankles down to thirty-eight slender knife toes, should become permanent body style. There are, maybe, two or three other steadfast body formations. . . .

Bugger Gang's home galaxy language—they spoke Red English—disappeared during fourth follow-up shake down. They had miraculously survived the burn-off—they didn't know then who started it, or where it came from. *They gazed at each other silently and discovered mind touch.* With alert curiosity they began to spread out their dreams on this planet, making trips—invented rituals for manhood and child organs—each one always certain distance longer than previous one. (Mind touch in discovery area to as many plants and animals as possible, make hunt of manhood, and return quickly to Homedirt.) All this led Bugger Gang to new friends and, more important, to terrestrial intelligent allies. . . .

It's late afternoon and sky is very clear. Yellow sun is still hot, but air is light and breezy. Small yet visible yellow particles are thrown off by sun, and reach so far because they're inside long slivers of light, which burst in the windy, free-roaming, dancing atmosphere surrounding this planet. These particles are released, free to be pushed, to fly, or float to living matter within gravitational field.

Unfortunately, now, they are like signs in a slave pen. They lead last, dying packs of vicious, terrestrial mob creatures to food and thought control. (These mobsters are the Cretin Brothers, who once were, for millions and millions of years, absolute rulers of dictatorship on this planet.) Most of them murdered each other during great burn-off. The remaining ones are blindies—they see only traces of yellow particles—and they eat anything across miles of space following raw length of chain and remembering turbulence of war.

And also these awful things still commit obscene practices of torture on plant and animal life, painfully extracting past thoughts and image-feelings with hard shocks of electric pressure pulsing tighter and tighter until juice is turned off at body center point inside tall, elegantly rooted leafgrain or eight-legged, savage, green toothlocker. . . .

Yellow mold grows slowly on doorways of old dreams floating mist of power gas and deadly weapons. Dark clouds of odor, memory bubbles, and heavy metal noise of flaming belts move through shadow alleys, time tunnels, and canals in ruins of secret city. And well within irregular gloomy shadows front legs scratch hairy fur on belly. . . .

Plants growing on few geometrical fields which dot this planet are set in three rows of low bushes. These are old time, static protection barriers. The bushes themselves are red, while plants, which grow out of them in series of concentric circles, shaped like arrow target, are a dull gray. Rows of bushes form crisscross lines on fields, and in centers of these crossing lines are machine towers of great height and bright yellow color—somehow metal has been treated to repel both visible and invisible rays of yellow sun. . . .

The two major land masses on this planet aren't very pretty to look at: colors are mostly yellow, gray or black, and sometimes green, blue or red. Sluggish yellow ocean forms oval band separating two continents. Ocean is seventy-five miles wide at all points. Strips of boulders, which create natural caves, and petrified rock vegetation connect two land forms every 350 miles, and also cut out ladder of oval shape dividing this planet into two nearly equal parts.

Bugger Gang lives on eastern shore of heavy metal sea, only other large, above-ground, body of water. To their east are successive bands of area: first, petrified forest zone, then region of yellow and gray geometric fields, next a green landscape with many yellow lines, really streams, scattered throughout, and finally airless desert in mixed colors of green, red and yellow. (Bugger Gang hasn't finished exploring this desert.)

All around sea at regular intervals of distance are ruins, violently mutilated fortifications, cities, and ports, most of which were destroyed before the night burn-off, and some even before Bugger Gang landed here. Packs of robot machines, built for all different purposes, roamed throughout this land belt until they were destroyed once and for all in burn-off. Bugger Gang had been able to demolish only twenty machines, fourteen robot protectors, and six mechanical terror monsters.

The strip of land which lies tangent to west shore of sea contains soft gray boulders, vacant lots, yellow mold on gnarled roots, deep burning pits, unbelievable smells, and the bones of many unknown animals.

Shadows from ageless filth, numberless dragonflies, and sperm devils, the giant beasts of this planet, hunt for decayed flesh and plants in this stretch of land.

Next in succession there's a wide land range of gray and red mountains with pitch black tunnels winding underneath. Then there are two tracts of land between yellow ocean and mountains: forest of rock vegetation with sections of warm sucking mud in black smell of decay, poisonous sky, burning pits, and pits brimful of stagnant yellow water, which doesn't even stir a ripple when anything is thrown into it. It swallows everything with a gulp, few air bubbles slightly breaking surface, and revolting smell seeping through the air attracting dragonflies and sperm devils.

In contrast, region of land leading to ocean shore luxuriates in old but sturdy yellow trees, patches of leafgrains, tallest, greenest plants of this planet, familiar haunted protection fields, yellow streams, and many friendly, and some intelligent, animals.

Bugger Gang was beginning to spread their dreams to penetrate gray and red mountains, but now two daring individuals, who aren't at all alike, are pushing their way into petrified forest....

Starbarf strokes what he has called since childhood his bow and arrow coming out of his chest. The arrow is especially pleasurable and relaxing to touch. He thinks over his future, wondering what he's trying to prove by passing set limits of his bugger journey. He's beginning to understand his own desires: he wants to be the greatest man in Bugger Gang. But he is not yet a man since he hasn't killed his first sperm devil.

His companion, his thought and knife brother, is called Ppssss: he's really an amphibian canoe animal. The two voyagers obviously aren't from the same race or for that matter the same species, but they work together like a man in a boat, as if they have established some bond which transcends need for speech. Mind touch.

"Ppssss, my brother, we should stop for a while and rest so our wounds may heal...."

When they started out from Homedirt, their life zone on this planet, there were eight bugger candidates: two boys with ripped-off noses replaced by razor-sharp wheel-blades on ends of petrified wood pipes, one boy without shoulders, shaped like battering ram with flat, thick piece of metal fitted into top of his head, Starbarf, and four fur-covered canoe animals.

The journey plan prepared for them by their elders was: ten weeks forced march to base of gray and red mountains—absolutely no hunting side trips at that time; next they split up into pairs, each one going into separate tunnel, and reuniting on other side of mountains; then return together for manhood hunt of sperm devil; kill one, remove its scales; and come back immediately to Homedirt.

While they were fighting off attack of dragonflies near burning pit in filth of west seashore, they took an oath that if they lived, they'd go all the way to yellow ocean mentioned many times in grim legends of canoe animals.

They thought of themselves as a small band of free men from a free land moving bravely but cautiously through slave territory.

They reached four tunnel openings in gray and red mountains. They paired off, one man with one canoe animal, and rode into separate subterranean countries of horror and lunacy.

The ground was covered with network of veins filtered through a green slime. Paddling was incredible difficult. The tunnels narrowed continuously at top and bottom. The rough stones burned Starbarf's feet when he was finally forced to walk. Ppssss searched for messages in darkest shadows. This seemed to rouse unspeakable things, bubbling in thick ooze all around the two frightened explorers.

Mind touch from canoe animal:

"O my brother, these drooling things were first people of this planet. Once they had giant shoulders, white skin in blue shadows, and pointed whip tails. They ruled benevolently. Light penetrated to the very core of this planet. The ocean water was clear and filled with rhythmic fish of beautiful motions, and full of music and harmonious scents. The lands were lush with yellow trees, leafgrains, older, more lovely plants, and uncountable species of well-fed, peaceloving animals. Then the Cretin Brothers drove first people into exile. And now, watch out! Their last home is in this foul slime. They can't sway back and forth even an inch because pain of vileness and corruption is so unbearable. But they still have slaves. . . .

Then there were four leaps into the dark. . . .

Then there were four glimpses into these unexplored dungeons of filth. . . .

Hundreds of dripping, two feet tall, slime beasties, the panic dwarfs and flesh seekers . . . they crawled out of stones and up through veins in the ground. . . .

These slaves attached themselves everywhere with sucker paws and pale yellow saliva dripped down small pointed chins. . . .

Slime, stones, and grizzly water poured into journey boys and spurted back out hungry teeth pigs, who immediately joined the fights. . . .

Bugger Gang and canoe animals didn't stand a chance, only Starbarf and Ppssss staggered out safely to other side of mountains, but they were covered with blood sores, teeth wounds, and needles. . . .

Starbarf is one of those incredibly energetic young men who seem sent by heaven to create disasters. His skin is mostly the color of dust in the summer sun. He radiates a vast driving force of will in rainstorms, and while others sleep, his head comes from many points and is welded together into geometric pattern: an intergalactic steam shovel.

He has been nominated by Bugger Council of Free Men and

Canoe Animal Brothers to become bow and arrow man when he attaches to his body scales of just-dead sperm devil—at important manhood ritual ceremony in Bugger Council Hall—and then he'll be able to contact noise in yellow stream. . . .

Starbarf and Ppssss waited three days for their brothers on far side of gray and red mountains until frenzy numbed their feelings, and long yellow claws appeared in their backs and dug into ground for spider towers. They decided again, in spite of huge faces and pieces of distance that might drift into their hair, to extend their bugger journey as far as possible. They thought they could twist together lands of black food and forget weaving memories of petrified body shapes. They would avoid poisonous lumps of yellow mold (as if that mattered) and never follow faint whiffs of decay like tortured animal meat on the wind.

They pushed on. . . .

If you've ever seen antique earth canoe with two eyes, three ears, and covered with fluffy pelt of rainbow-tipped gray fur, then you know what Ppssss looks like. He's descendant from long line of delicate hues (broken mental pictures) and gravity shadows of mad silence. He vibrates and moves things by looking at them backwards. His body is flexible and he can roll himself into a ball of sleep. Arms can appear close to his mouth whenever necessary. And he will dance and shuffle, poring out through fur black liquid sweat, when Cretin Brothers are notched in score of his dim past.

For all his people landing of Bugger Gang was benefit and protection for sky affairs. Now they can caress each other and stroke out encrusted odors and whiffs of mold and petrified decay.

The canoe animal's triangular eyes look around for campsite. If possible he doesn't want to race across these sunbaked stones. His race had been originally built from rotten splinters of wood. He mournfully watches stagnant yellow pool. His sides ache when he's been out of fresh water too long.

Meanwhile Starbarf chokes as if he's sick, ate too much waste, grabs his circular feet thinking he may need to swim. Red and yellow cliffs in distance behind him are very distracting. They stand out. His heart pounds towards yellow ocean. He jumps up for dream hatching in slow metal fire, stands back and cuts the air. It falls with a loud crash.

Starbarf leaps inside his canoe animal brother. They decide to rest under overcoat, which isn't far away. It's one of the few that fell out of yellow sky on appearance long ago of Bugger Gang ship. It's surrounded by half-healed flesh, architecture, other body alterations, empty metal parts, and unusual bizarre limbs of stone forest.

But inside they feel sheltered, untroubled, and levelheaded, and are tickled by meandering yellow stream. Gray blue fringes of coat expand in warm breeze. They touch each other's mind.

"We couldn't have found a more perfect place for campsite."

Ppssss picks up with backward glance seamy vest, which talks in color blasts, then he disappears with it into depths of overcoat pocket, source of the steam. Starbarf's face melts and runs down his long neck. He'll have to repair it. He rummages through bleeding formations of crystal, puts flat-topped stone and peg on his steam shovel head, hangs new face on peg, sits down cross-legged, and waits.

A wide-winged patch of color bursts in the sky. Silent, broken wheels are indistinguishable in this shallow land, but jissom trails are difficult to move or conceal.

Starbarf's perfectly still underneath overcoat, vibrating in his head sensations of friendship and good will, also rearranging his face, broadcasting latest news, putting in new exchange of ideas, and hoping to catch wave thought beams of mind touch in dusty air.

He doesn't have long to wait.

A front paw hand is dragged through dirt. It stretches out by instinct and is capable of bursting into twenty eye-teeth. Black eyes flick motionlessly towards overcoat, ears twitch nervously, blunt nose wrinkles, and mental pictures form, although they aren't needed.

Something is already in Starbarf's brain counting rooms where dates and figs grow in abundance. Ten blasts of light jump from rock to rock. Seamy cloth collapses in burst of heat, then explodes into color vapors that move across ground like network of fine wires.

Starbarf continues to touch his own mind. He's waiting for his body to split down the middle. He doesn't try to withdraw from mutations. Wires turn up at edges of his eyes. His memory lines blur beneath his feet. He's ready to touch a rhunag, smallest intelligent creature on this planet. It loves to change shape to collect information and make trades through immediate color flashes or else long-term agreements.

Starbarf feels rhunag moving closer. Electric crackle of sound and brilliant explosion of light disturb yellow stream. He doesn't move any part of his body. But it was only after many hard years on this planet that Bugger Gang taught themselves virtue of patience. (They had been too nervous in uncharted regions of deep space, in vast mind-consuming nexus of outer galaxies, and in barren lands that time forgot warmed by alien suns.)

Rays of light leap out of yellow stream. Colors aren't used as weapons or to shout war-cry with great exuberance of triumph. Starbarf's mind is laughing, summer has returned to his lips. The rhunag touches him without icy breath of complete nothingness!

Intelligence meets intelligence.

It's a moment of dull joy and vast hopes. . . .

Untidy piles of dried and shriveled fruit are in front of Starbarf's feet. He turns on his head. His numerous toes separate into shovels, dig towards this treasure, but stop halfway.

Ten billion stars have lined up unnoticed. Gravity shadows bend around every spark of light, and colors merge with aging roots.

Slavery and remnants of older dark race are discussed. Everyone hates the Cretin Brothers. Secret western city is mentioned more than once. Curiosity hides its own purposes. Rhunags have their own form of intelligence, although it might not be compared with that of humans. Empty space doesn't interest them at all.

This rhunag still has shocks of intensity from day before yesterday. It has traveled a long way. It had exchanged softening meat flesh for fading dead eyes in the air. Now it wants to deliver three more loads of fruit.

A further trade would take place in fifty years. It would be responsibility of Bugger Gang Council. It will involve hundreds of different wires, land stretching between two yellow streams, and thousands of gray feathered wings that will have been accumulated through dancing. Both parties are pleased with their bargains....

Ppssss splashes back from bottom of pocket. The air is smoky, and wonderful yellow afterglow begins to fade in sky. He's carrying fish which twists and shakes in its last dying spasms. Starbarf considers blood stains on his brother's ghost hands with speechless amazement.

Fierce cry rings out, then roar echoes through short line of red and yellow cliffs that moves rapidly towards protective overcoat. Dusky forms creep out of rocks on all sides!

Ppssss forms message in the air:

"O my brother, there are no more hunting grounds in your feet. That fish is the last one."

But Starbarf doesn't look confused.

"Ppssss, take the baskets of fruit. Let's go! Danger touches my mind."

They leave protection of overcoat. Starbarf climbs into his canoe animal brother and paddles over gray rocks. They look back once and see red and yellow cliffs push their way to overcoat, which is flopping helplessly on wet hard ground, and tear it into hundreds of pieces.

Two explorers now have specific destination: ancient secret city of Cretin Brothers across yellow ocean. Both feel more strongly renewed sense of destiny in their bugger journey. They want to add more than just an inch or two to their phallic images on Bugger Council walls back in Homedirt.

They move cautiously through sickening yellow-gray rocks and petrified forest, always on lookout for dragonflies and sperm devils. Caution has been drilled into them with a steam shovel. Bugger Gang isn't master of this planet, they're only outlaws for Red Terrestrial Galaxy. They have no weapons that can whip out small, yellow meteors to explode and form continuous line of deadly monster gas.

The canoe animals are their one true ally, energetic like old yellow trees, powerful, circumspect, and audacious, real salt of the earth. With Bugger Gang they exterminate, whenever possible, dragonflies and sperm devils. But they have only recently come out of their water homes, when burn-off heated sea beyond their endurance. They're still a small tribe and prefer to live in caves near good size body of water. They can make small amounts of fetid water fresh again, and need salt everyday to survive. They seem to know a great deal about Cretin Brothers and their ruined cities.

Who are these Cretin Brothers with their traditions of monstrous slavery and dark beginnings in experimental pigpens of an even older race?

They are worst degenerates of degenerate civilization, but that civilization has fallen into a heap of shit and has so far never recovered. They were makers of deformed, unspeakable weapons, creators of the dragonflies and infamous sperm devils. Only several hundred of them still exist, and these can no longer produce more than one offspring. On this planet females become more fruitful as their mates kill more and more of their enemies. Since Cretin Brothers have lost knowledge to control ageless, devil-raging weapons, their women have become almost barren.

Two centuries ago this planet was wracked by a series of devastating, smelly wars. Cretin Brothers jumped on each other's backs. It had started in their teeth. Vague, uneasy recollections quickly gave way to fury. (Home Clusters were gutted and burned. City bombed city. Colorless vapors settled on every spacefield. Their skin, which was thicker than bark of ancient trees, and flesh, which was as hard as scales of sperm devils, were gashed open and yellow drek, their life force, oozed out their veins at incredible rate. Minds were short-circuited and washed like laundry. Panic dwarfs and flesh seekers growling with pleasure creeped out of ground to sniff flesh and bones turned to jelly and eat warriors dying on soft wings.)

With endless despair Cretin Brothers continued to kill each other off. Their ribs shattered, their legs broke, and their jaws were crushed. All energy was lost in mystery of warm flesh and determination to torture. Crumpled pieces of cloth flapped in the wind. Rusty vegetation didn't hesitate to burst through their heads, but no fear of death roared in their hearts protected by now featureless bodies.

Then the giant burn-off came.

Irresistible mass of flame fell on almost every part of this planet....

Cretin Brothers seemed to be paralyzed, only their muscles quivered with dim certainty. They aimlessly turned around and around, dizzy in licking red flames as if they had become blind through frenzied storm of anger and madness.

Only few packs of Cretin Brothers survived, but their corporate blood had become thin and rotten....

Now they come out of their ruined cities in small bands to search for food and knowledge of their lost weapons. They follow network of chains filtered through yellow particles. They destroy plant and animal life in the most despicable ways. This is their only pleasure or torture, but it also means of gathering information....

Ppssss slides along the ground looking for gravity shadows that might contain messages. There are wide fissures between some petrified trees. Ancient machines burn slowly. Fires flicker in the depths. He stops to listen, and then thinks of something important but his words trail off into silence that seems to be slightly menacing. He's nervous....

Mind touch.

"O my brother, runners in the dark! A horde of tarcoolies are on the move!"

"Unbelievable!"

Tarcoolies are sticky long black stones with yellowish brown fur ball at each end. They are noted for stubbornly clinging to one particular place generation after generation. They meet any danger with brainless ferocity that doesn't comprehend fear except for Cretin Brothers.

There have been forerunners all night carrying piles of boxes. A jissom trail has warned them. It was torn loose from the ground and rolled into narrow crack of fire.

Starbarf takes out one of his eyes and tries to listen to it. He gestures inpatiently. He once thought he possessed a thousand eyes whenever he wanted them, but now he feels spasms of flying dust and fiery needles swagger down his legs.

He stares at his canoe animal brother, who has become absorbed in sticky pieces of fur. Ppssss is getting the information. His body displays no readable emotion, although sensations of distaste are plain along the edges of his gray fur. Then he shuffles through some dirt in curious little half dance which betrays his agitation as much as his thoughts can.

Mind touch.

"O my brother, the tarcoolies are hunting for feathers and pieces of hair. They say they've seen some Cretin Brothers. This strip of land was once a cretin garden. It had a formal structure. They told me we're going in right direction for ancient ruins of secret city, straight ahead across yellow ocean.

"They also said that there's a gap between your teeth large enough for a feather. And when I told them your name they threw up."

Starbarf points his left hand to the north, his right hand to the west, and his other hand, which is between his legs, strokes bow and arrow coming out of his chest. He takes off its protective casing. The arrow shakes.

But isn't it more than just an arrow?: it is his manhood, his maker of babies, as well as deadly weapon. Its jissom is poison acid, fatal to touch for everyone on this planet, except, of course, females of Bugger Gang.

And now closer bonds between Bugger Gang and their brothers has made acid jissom less deadly for canoe animals: in three or four life durations it's expected that the two species will be able to mate and produce children.

As a weapon bugger child organ is very effective, especially against sperm devils, which bugger gangsters, after they become men, try to kill on sight whenever and wherever possible.

The jissom kills by burning through soft flesh—it's corrosive acid—and then its poison goes to work on internal organs and arteries. Even largest sperm devils, some of whom grow to be sixty feet long, die horrible deaths within five minutes after bugger jissom burns through.

The bow, which grows out of gangster's chest, is used to shoot acid jissom over long distances. Its effective range is 250 yards. It's really just a bone. Bowstring is made from small bits of flesh twisted and hooked together. Foreskin of arrow or child organ is wrapped around middle of bow. Part of skin is cut off during bugger ceremony after gangster has killed his first sperm devil: this improves the jissom range. The arrow itself is always hard and also doesn't move.

To shoot jissom poison bugger gangster must pull back flesh bowstring with all three of his hands, then let go. Bowstring, which is very taut, moves along arrow (ten sperm producing balls, like cluster of grapes, are inside gangster's chest near his two hearts) and pushes jissom out at tremendous speed....

Starbarf stops stroking his arrow. He feels satisfied. Yellow sun is rising and it makes plain every possible hand and foot. Ppssss looks for echoes of dust and showers of blue sparks. He hesitates for moment before long broken stretch of bare rock. Starbarf jumps into him. His oval, grim body turns around slowly a few times....

After this short rest they start their journey again. They hope they're near new land zone, but they really don't know. They move along swiftly. It has taken many long years of hard practice for canoe animals to learn how to travel quickly.

They keep sharp lookout as they paddle their way through dirty rocks. This is just the type of land to harbor dragonflies. And while those pests are small, their lightning-swift attack from above makes them foes not to be disregarded. But only flying things they see are two shadows with graceful, lovely, delicate wings. They're like two flickering spots in morning sky of great depth and peacefulness.

The morning fades into afternoon, then into long hot twilight of this planet, and still Starbarf and Ppssss haven't stopped. It has been rough going, but at least they haven't come across traces of Cretin Brothers. There are no domes, ruins of isolated castles, no two-horned machines, or monorail tracks, no discarded tools, power wagons, or weapons, nor any other relics that you might find very easily near Homedirt.

This wide open land must have been product of busy imagination supplying life to various kinds of rocks. But great plans had exploded with insect monster machines. All the message shadows are shivering but quiet. Breath of inexhaustible life is in grip of terror. Memories of wickedness are still lying about.

Starbarf turns his head. His unblinking eyes stare at tunnel of yellow-green glass. Dreams of ambition and admiration connect him with finest Bugger Gang legends. He sees visions of beautiful world under warm yellow light. High ceiling is over his head and very simple glass archway is starting to form behind him.

Waiting lust hunger forms in tangle of closing planes. Beast thing leaps into yellow-green dome. Too late for poison jissom. Starbarf's free hand caresses the hair. Cold harsh life rushes into his belly.

Little waves start up through canoe animal's body. Ppssss finally realizes dangerous undercurrents. He makes quick getaway from thought dome. It almost cuts off his tail end.

Mind relaxes and touches Starbarf.

"O my brother, that was close. Thought dome turns your mind to the wall. I hadn't known any were left, unless, maybe this is a new one. We would have been in misery for weeks until last tasty morsel."

They're quiet for long time. Starbarf remembers stories about terror robots which might still protect some destroyed cities. Bugger Gang's intergalactic space ship, most precious object they owned, had been torn apart by squad of terror monsters ten hours after they landed on this planet. Those machines had many flexible snippers, blades, and shovel arms.

They're almost in ocean border zone. They head little bit north to attract a wind, hoping to discover water, preferably yellow stream made by all animals of this area. Then Ppssss would be able to touch out more information about current events.

They come upon what looks like large cradle. Several animals are inside it making grunting noises. As is usual with most animals on this planet, who aren't intelligent, they stink to high heaven. They're trying to stretch their heads off. Not one flying creature is in sight.

Animals in cradle jump out: two throgs, green toothlocker, and five windhogs. Other animals replace them. There are at least fifty standing in line nearby. There's always someone in the cradle, and there are never any serious fights.

Yellow liquid pours out ten holes in bottom of cradle: this is the source of fresh stream.

Destruction has stiffened animal shoulders a mile or two beyond conjectured jissom trail. Most of them stay away from there. Rain and trembling rocks haven't returned to heavy molten bodies. True as day animals make life interesting for two wanderers.

Ppssss slides into water, how he loves pure animal stream. Even Starbarf splashes in ankle deep for sheer pleasure of feeling yellow liquid curl around his three legs once more.

They move downstream and pass small islands of animal waste, swept together in neat piles, some showing multicolored plant life, and others the decayed, foul activities of Cretin Brothers, who use their waste to torture and extract information from both plants and animals. It burns through the skin, and slowly, painfully petrifies the body. While that's happening, plant or animal's mind releases all images and thoughts of its past life. When it reaches neutral memory point, creature dies, turned to stone.

Cretin Brothers record these mind death image rattles on special thought impression tapes because they can't understand or use mind touch. They can also get information from all kinds of water, except yellow animal liquid where venomous waste material isn't able to sink. It floats for several days then dissolves, leaving black film on water, which disappears altogether in two weeks.

Night floats into the water. Scented shrubbery showers petals into yellow stream. Starbarf plants his rectum leg in animal waste island, crosses his other two legs, and sits down.

In few minutes he'll be ready to eat, then sleep through night, but first he digs out his own waste material from its sack under his chin. He casually throws it into yellow stream because there's no need to bury it here. It will sink. Actually only reason Bugger Gang bury its waste on this planet is to prevent Cretin Brothers from finding it and gaining valuable information.

Ppssss has stayed in yellow stream and touches all animal thoughts and images as they come and go. Once he touches raging hunger of dragonflies. Tightness pervades their heads towards other animals and they snarl. Another time he touches memory of windhog nest invaded by thoughtless sperm devils: cries of help unanswered, invisible death skin on mass of red flames, running sores, burning flesh and hair, and escape of one windhog.

After eating Starbarf strokes his arrow for pleasure. Thin sheet of blood and thrill spreads through his body. He shivers. Stream of jissom—arching line of sapphire and ruby sparks—streaks up towards black darkness of night....

Then a smell so vivid, so menacing, so alien, so full of germs and disgust, brings Starbarf to his feet. It's something growing outside his field of mind touch. It doesn't reply. It's protected from gravity shadows. It moves very quickly. It has tremendous energy, strongest Starbarf has yet encountered on this planet. It forces him to throw up.

He runs down to yellow water. He feels canoe animal's bewilderment at odor added to nausea and alarm.

Mind touch from yellow water:

"Danger! Danger! Danger!"

Danger has crossed the night, from east to west, an odor, a trail returning to secret place. What had it come from? Why was it moving so quickly? And what was going to happen now?

WHY I LIKE TO WRITE?!

I like to write because I feel a deep need within me every night to express my love and abiding interest in mankind. Each man, woman, and child deserves to be the subject of a great story. I wish I had more time, less sleep.

Give me a pill and I will tell you that all men are essentially different—in their passions, their outlooks, their looks, their views of themselves and others, in their beliefs, their jokes, their interests, and their sex problems. THIS IS EXACTLY THE REASON WHY I'd rather write about men and women than write about buildings, machines, or art objects.

Whenever I sit down at my desk to write a story I always try to keep in mind the parts men play as individuals, not as mere abstractions, in the universe which surrounds them. THIS IS EXACTLY THE THING that gives history its true and proper value, poetry *some* of its merit, and stories that I write THEIR ONLY REASON FOR EXISTING.

FIRST COMPLETED PASS OF THE DAY

The sun through a haze sticks to the tar and concrete, it burns the back of my neck. I go over to the play yard with two basketballs, a football, volleyball, two whiffle bats, three whiffle balls, and *Lyubka The Cossack and other stories*, by Issac Babel, in a cardboard box, one corner of it ripped halfway down.

I open two small gates on 88th Street. It's one o'clock, drowsy Sunday afternoon, distant sounds of traffic. I watch a fat little man walk quickly down the block. He's hugging a blue pillow against his chest. Several puerto rican kids in torn shirts are following him. He stops at the corner and glances back over his shoulder. And the kids start chattering in puerto rican.

I pick up dented metal lids and set them on empty garbage cans chained to the fence. Incinerator dust and broken glass. I am listening to a song on the radio. A girl in dungaree shorts is sitting next to it. Her eyes are closed and her face is pointed up to the sun. She is waiting for her friends. Her legs are dirty, suntanned, and shining with sweat. Her knees are rough like the skin of oranges. I see her every week with her friends, but they never come into the yard.

Lines for the basketball court, the bases for whiffleball, the foul lines, and pitcher's mound are painted a bright yellow. I put the box down next to flagpole and take halfcourt jump shot. Two kids are yelling at me through the fence to open up gate on 87th Street. Ball misses by a mile. I open the big green gate.

The taller kid in a red short sleeve shirt—he looks around sixteen, with a mop of dark curly hair—races across the yard and scoops up the football.

I start to walk back to pick up the basketball.

The quarterback stands over an imaginary center and barks out the signals. Team down. Set. He sizes up the opposition's defense. I'm playing deep safety, but I really want to play offensive end and catch the ball and run all the way for a touchdown.

I whistle to the quarterback as I run in, fake with my head to the outside, and cut across the middle. Fifteen yards into enemy territory and I'm wide open.

"Hut one. Hut two. Hut three."

The ball is snapped. I'm waving my arms. The quarterback backpedals four or five quick stops, cocks his arm, and lets go with the long bomb to his friend, who's all alone behind the goal line near the gate, which is the right corner of our touch football field.

The receiver shields his eyes with one hand, gets under the ball, and makes a perfect touchdown catch.

Our eyes meet while I'm cheering for him and clapping my hands. But then he takes off with the ball like a halfback up 87th Street. A tiny sound pops out of my throat. My eyes roll back. The tall passer splits out to 88th Street.

I stand flatfooted in middle of empty yard shaking my head at first completed pass of the day. . . .

from
HELPING THE GUY WITH THE PROSTITUTES

Part Five:

> Crazy truckdriver, feeling for life, perfect blow job, Saliva's room, sadness of dawn, Jesse's girl rule, breath choking fuck desire, slippery mouth, telephone, raw wind, seismographic seizure, drinking stories, bright blue sky.

He had the biggest goddam stomach I'd ever seen, this crazy, early-rising truckdriver, who's standing barefoot naked in middle of hall, taking large swigs of gin, beating his lump of a head against the wall, grabbing, pulling on his dick, and then hopping giant steps with it towards the elevator.

Jesse and I took it easy for a second, watching—me punching my thighs, Jesse stooped over, last puff on cigarette, hand reaching under elevator stool, and both of us grinning silly at these mad dog antics, the leaping, prancing, falling down slobbering drunk.

We had rushed up in elevator to protect Jesse's property, the girls, all of them Mexican of various ages, sizes, and shapes.

The truckdriver roared out in husky, drinker's voice, a voice of thunder, a persistent rumbling, like pounding of storm against rocks, or ceaseless roar of some headlong attack from out of the infinite. . . .

His clothes lay in a heap on rusty fire extinguisher isolated in silent heart of city.

The air was filled with dust rising from floor. . . .

So fucking awful drunk, almost hearing his brains snap, swept up into some whirling vortex of dizziness, now he's facing the wall still holding his dick: long bellyful crystal jet of piss smacked against dirty red wallpaper and rippled down to floor in two or three dark streams.

"That motherfuckin' cocksucker," was all Jesse said. He was all over feeling good and was getting plenty pissed off.

Jesse, he's a quiet sort of guy, doesn't say much, just uses five or six curse words to say what he means. Only likes to talk at any great length about his prostitutes and best ways to treat (fuck) them.

The highstrung truckdriver reared up like a horse, snorting and neighing, before old Jesse took him down with long piece of pipe he keeps under his elevator stool.

I was choking with some indefinable sorrow when I looked down at that workingman spread out on the dusty floor. Pearly drops of sperm. His eyes like holes wide open in the void. His mouth's tight shut, lips colorless, and blood spurted out his ears.

It struck me that he was just harmless maniac with real feeling for life, a kind of angel idiot with body of a pig. Never had a perfect blow job before, just led truckdriver's life with regular job, big meals, and a little crime. Few minutes ago probably rejoicing about the wonderfulness of it all, hopes of excitement and flesh larger than life, holy flowers bursting in his head.

Jesse and I dragged him back into Saliva's room, where he had been touched out of his mind with joy, yelling "sonofabitch" and "for chrissakes," dancing an endless dance of nakedness, phewing, slapping his knee, and wiping the sweat out of his crotch.

Saliva, the best blow job expert of all Jesse's girls was acting up hysterical fit of complete agony, naked, racing back and forth from bed to narrow writing table where she kept six pack of beer, two smoky thumbprint glasses, a phone, and some clean blue towels.

She had called down to desk clerk, Frankie—Mexican, smooth fat face with pencil line mustache and small gray eyes—who told her right away to take it easy.

"We're coming," I yelled at her through the phone.

She's crying and ripped out of her mind that this cretin potbellied jerk had gone hog wild when his flood of hot sperm shot into her wide night-dark mouth. . . .

Outside Houston the sun was starting to rise. Saliva's room was filled with shadows, giving a feeling of overpowering sadness to the beginning of day and to the end of our night. . . .

Jesse's eyes glittered in a mask of blood-spattered dust.

I was combing my hair.

The senseless, beef-brained truckdriver was dead between the ears, out cold like a light. Now his tongue hanging out his mouth white and disgusting, teeth were stained green, grease on his nose, hair dried out, and gray muck in the corners of his eyes.

A fly settled on my comb and crawled along it. . . .

Two rats, bleeding in their death agony, rolled into the middle of the room, the one on the bottom screaming so desperately that I had to turn my head away. . . .

This guy was garbage. A drop of blood on his forehead. We dumped him under the bed. . . .

My thoughts drifted away, out the window into cool Monday dawn of Houston, rustling in an occasional breeze, then back again, where they joined forces with Jesse's one track thought waves.

In two seconds I was on fire with enthusiasm.

Jesse forced three of his fingers up Saliva's ass hole. She jumped up, spit—left it hanging on her chin—and hollered for him to let her go. But I put a quick end stop to her dribble with my fists sailing into her brown soft tits.

Jesse had taught me well the perfect girl rule of business: when one of the girls don't like what you're doing, punch her as hard as you can where it counts, then she'd sure like it okay.

Jesse picked up Saliva one-handed and slapped her down hard on the writing table. He knocked over a chair. Six pack of beer fell on the floor. His hand popped out her ass. She rolled over. I grabbed a towel and pretend to dry my hands and face clean.

Tears from the fearful anguish and endless rush of womanly pain grew in the corners of her green eyes then rolled down her burning cheeks. The palms of her trembling hands were sweaty. The unspeakable loneliness of self-pity that is blind and dumb rose up hot in her pussy.

She hopelessly shook her head. Her body quivering and senseless on the table.

Light filtered through the dirty window. Stars grew paler and paler in early morning sky.

I snatched up a can of beer, opened it, threw some in Saliva's face to wake things up, then drained the can and wiped my mouth with the back of my hand.

This gave my head a sudden flash picture of whole life ahead of me that could never be explained or understood by any head shrink or intellectual social welfare creep.

I picked up Houston with one hand and calmly put it in my pocket....

I tried to clear the thickness from my seething brain as I watched Saliva's shoulders go up in a shrug that means everything from total ignorance to infinite understanding.

The beast in Jesse was up and raging. He was mastered by the sheer surging of life, the tidal wave of being, the perfect joy of each separate muscle, joint, and sinew totally on fire, expressing itself in movement, soaring exultantly through the stars and over the face of dead matter that doesn't move.

Saliva opened her mouth wide as Jesse shoved in there his stiff cock of immense proportions....

Life streamed through him in a bursting flood, a wild passion, until it seemed that it would tear him apart in dazzling ecstasy and pour out generously over the world. . . .

Then his senses were fainting, fading, falling, and dying slowly away. . . .

Suddenly that dizzy pride destroying heart shakiness and breath choking fuck desire hit me square in my manhood.

I opened the trapdoor of my mind. . . .

I had to get between Saliva's legs and fill up my total self with the incredible deep beauty and complete unearthly loveliness of her gaping pussy. . . .

Spasms of delight plunged through my body. . . .

I rolled off the table, one glass fell and cracked on the floor. I staggered to the bed, every muscle in my body shattered as my mind cooled down and recovered from the intoxication of fucking.

I lay on the wrinkled bed, the damp come stains, and pubic hairs. I stared into the blank shadows, then watched the light of dawn appear like a dirty yellow smear, a trickle of liquid mud, on the windowpane.

Jesse was ready for his second takeover action. . . .

He pushed his hands hard into Saliva's shoulders as he mounted her struggling pussy.

He was like a gray shadow gliding between the sign of night and the whisper of dawn, bouncing on the desk, grunting and storming in his exertion, waiting for the white blaze of heat, the mystery sunburst of light to red through his head and burn out his body—the exploding of the seed, the running of the sap—then he'd fall through the universe again. . . .

Meanwhile I got off my lazy ass, remembered something, went over to the telephone, rang up Frankie, and told him to send up two porters to cart away truckdriver.

Jesse and I were too busy working out important business transactions.

Frankie moaned that all he could do downstairs was beat off his meat like he's a butcher or something, and he's feeling waves of sickness rumble through his stomach and into his damp thighs.

I related this miserable news to Jesse, who stopped acting up business for a moment—wild blank stare fading, eyes start blinking—and took phone from me to tell Frankie that he, Frankie, would turn black like a nigger if he didn't cut out playing with himself.

Jesse tossed phone back to me to hang up. Jolly face, snorts of laughter, then he's saying Saliva's cunt was nothing next to her slippery mouth.

I said her vagina was like a dark quivering hunk of jelly.

Jesse nodded his head, pacing back and forth holding his hard black prick with both hands.

I asked Saliva if there's anyone in particular she wanted to phone up and talk to.

I looked her pussy right in the eye, my body pulsating with life, my mind aching with the mad desire to do something great.

She didn't answer.

I dialed seven numbers at random and heard the phone ring in somebody's house in Houston.

Then I rammed telephone up Saliva's earth-mother cunt. I saw in my mind's eye the abyss of incurable madness that would last forever in the Womb of Time.

Saliva groveled on the table, writhing in silent torment.

She screamed, her cry bursting upward in a great heartbreaking rush, dying down into trembling misery and bursting up again with rush upon rush of endless grief.

She puked up blood, raw egg, jisson stuck in her throat from fifty men, worms, chewing tobacco, kotex, and crank case oil.

Jesse grabbed Saliva in his arms and they danced together what he called his "victory dance," but very careful not to let ringing phone drop out her snatch.

Breathing heavy he was worked up to dreadful fury of sex, wooly hair sweating, wild gestures of his prick as he sucked in her body with eyes smoldering like coals of fire.

He threw her on the table again, almost tripping over telephone wire, ran his hand between her legs, then shoved vibrating black cock into her delicious mouth, blood-red lips grown full over strong white teeth, like burst of passion, the stirrings of the unconscious.

Jesse rubbed her pussy juice on his chest, belly, thighs, screw on sour face, threw it away.

I picked up empty glass, lean my ear on it under Saliva's belly button, sexy pubic hair line, listening to phone ring until I heard:

"Hello! Hello!" echo in her womb. "Who the hell's calling me so goddam early in the morning," rasped a sleep voice. "The sun's rising. I'm worn out working twelve hours a day. Need to get my fucking sleep."

I pulled out the phone. Glass shattered on the floor.

Jesse yelled from hard teeth deep into his dick.

All of a sudden I felt cold, as if I were standing out in raw wind in a thin shirt with no jacket on.

I walked in circles, kicked dead rats, shoulders hunched, hands deep in pockets, waiting for mind escape. Nothing exists. I glanced at Jesse, saw the yearning of immortality, delirious ecstasy spread over his face, ripping apart every fiber of his being.

Complete forgetfulness in this crashing, rending, throbbing of awakening life.

His body twitching in strange rippling waves as he screamed out loud:

"Fuck! ... Fuck! ... Fuck! ..."

I watched the seismographic seizure of fuck knife through his glistening body. . . .

They both fell together off the table. Saliva choking on Jesse's sweet load. Broken glass stuck in their bodies.

Jesse's knocked completely out, blasted into exhausted pleasure of restfulness—like me he had caught little sleep the night before.

A sign pulsed through the thick air like premonition of movement in a motionless void.

Saliva snarled and whimpered in her unconsciousness.

I bent over them to pull out Jesse's prick—up to the hilt in Saliva's foaming mouth—not to give her chance to tear it off in dreamless sleep.

Sperm dripped out corner of her lips onto sliver of glass. . . .

The fatigue of hopelessness and age crept into Jesse's face. . . .

I climbed into bed as two porters came in rubbing their sleepy eyes. They stood still for minutes, mouths dropped open in blank amazement, taking in our life-death sex scene.

Then they did their job with crazy stories to tell wine drinking buddies swirling in their heads. They moved bed over with me in it, doing things quietly, afraid Jesse or Saliva might come to and eat them up.

They struggled with two-ton body of truckdriver, couldn't lift it off floor. One of them whispered suggestion to get a wheelbarrow. The other guy shook his head "No." Finally they dragged him away, one on each arm. . . .

I looked through the window.

Daylight buzzed behind my tired brown eyes warm and heavy, exceedingly warm and heavy. . . .

Thought to write New York letter to girlfriend soon. . . .

Gray dusty streets under bright blue sky. . . .

SOMEBODY'S ALWAYS WINNING
for Ted Berrigan

Mr. Dominic Grotti was born and raised in New York City. He was named after his rugged grandfather, who came over here in the early 1880s. His father, Albert (Diamond Nose) Grotti, did alright for himself, and lived all his life on 107th Street. He was one of the founders of the very profitable 107th Street Social Club. The present Mr. Grotti is 48 years old with a full head of black hair and big eyes set far apart. He hasn't any brothers and two sisters are married and two are dead. His height is close to six feet and he weighs one hundred and ninety-five pounds. Forces of gravity have started pulling on his stomach, but his shoulders, chest, arms and legs are still built powerfully solid.

Mr. Grotti ... he's a smart businessman, but he isn't at all like those Wall St. bigshots. He doesn't own a two-family house on half a hundred acres in Scarsdale, although he could easily afford it, or shelter himself on the thirty-fourth floor of a Park Avenue luxury castle. Twelve years ago he took over an insurance business in Yorkville and for the past nine he's been living in the neighborhood—a large, expensively furnished ground floor apartment, both sides of the building, 350 East 87th Street, 2nd and 1st Avenues—with his wife, who's eleven years younger than him, and two children, a daughter, 10, and a son, 7. His house is located between another five-story apartment building, 348, and the three-story Oates Funeral Home with a red canopy. Facade of his building is painted grayish blue up to the second floor, there isn't any stoop to speak of, and no iron gates protect his windows.

Late one night a burglar broke into Mr. Grotti's apartment through the street window. A glass panel door separates the bedroom from the front livingroom.

Mr. Grotti woke up and heard the burglar's feet moving slowly towards the bedroom. He quietly shook his wife's shoulder and whispered into her ear, "Mary, don't make a sound, there's a thief in the livingroom." A tiny sound almost popped out of her throat. "Take it easy, and do exactly what I tell you to do. Ask me straight out, but in a regular voice, where I get all my money from. I'll tell you to mind your own business. Then act suspicious and ask me how come I never talk to you about the insurance policies I'm always selling. And say that you don't like the looks of the people who work for me and the strange hours they come over to the house. No matter what I do keep pestering me for answers."

Mrs. Grotti is a smart lady. She started kissing her husband and rubbing his hair. "Dear, are you awake?" she asked. Grunting noises. Mr. Grotti was breathing heavily. "Something's been bothering me for a long time, Dominic, and I want to get it straightened out right this minute."

An overdose of fear rushed through the livingroom. The burglar froze in his tracks. He widened his permanently bloodshot eyes and his fingers were sticky and trembling.

"What is it?" A hint of bad temper in Mr. Grotti's abrupt voice.

"Well, I know we're doing pretty good . . ." Her hands stroked his unshaven face and neck and she kissed him a few more times until he jerked his head back and told her, "Cut it out! What you want from me, woman, waking me up in the middle of the night? It had better be important."

"Well, I know we're doing pretty good," she repeated as though trying to recall a quickly memorized speech. "But what I want to know is, where does all the money come from? I'm married to you twelve years and I still don't understand what kind of insurance you sell. I'm positive we don't own any policies, and it's very embarrassing just to shrug my shoulders when the kids ask me why does daddy have so many baseball bats in the trunk of his car? . . . I'd like to know the answer to that too."

The burglar slowly moved his hand to his back pocket, touching the outlines of a long knife and a .25 caliber revolver. The knife was closed and there weren't any bullets in the gun's chamber. He could smell the sweat in his armpits. Drops rolled down his ribs and were absorbed by his dark shirt. He was a 29-year-old junkie, who was waiting for the next thing to happen.

Mr. Grotti inched away from his wife, turned his back to her and pulled the sheet and bedspread up to his neck. He made senseless noises in the blue shadows then his voice rang out with startling clearness.

"Listen, Mary, what a man does is his own business. I bring home plenty of money for you and the kids, and I work hard for it. You have everything you want and even more than that. Aren't both of the kids going to good Catholic schools? And didn't I buy you a mink coat and a new washing machine in the last few months?"

"That's not the point, Dominic!" She sat up and examined the back of his head. And she could feel the burglar breathing down her neck from the livingroom. She swallowed some saliva before continuing:

"Around six months ago I overheard two old ladies gossiping in the supermarket about you and your neighborhood business interests. I was right behind them. I tried not to listen but I couldn't help myself . . . I was stuck there."

"Oh yeah! Sure! I bet!" Mr. Grotti roared and threw off the covers. "What did the nosy bitches say?" There was anger and astonishment in his voice. He rolled over towards his wife but didn't look up at her face.

Mrs. Grotti stared straight ahead at a familiar blank screen of secrecy near the foot of the bed. Images gone over a hundred times before floated out of the mattress. They increased their speed, and once started nothing could scatter them . . . like a thousand-piece jigsaw puzzle completed almost instantly by a computer. Mrs. Grotti shivered and locked her arms around her knees. Then she spoke to her husband, and for the first time in many years she heard her voice molding each word clearly and scornfully.

"Yes . . . I remember all the details, it's like a movie, as a matter of fact, everything's still technicolor and bright lights in my hair. I was standing on the express line in Bohack's with three items, a gallon of milk, Turkish coffee, and a can of tomato paste. I was wearing my brown suede coat with the fur collar, just coming back from lunch with Jeannie, my closest high school friend, who was visiting New York for a holiday vacation with her third husband, Steve Harte, from Detroit. . . . Don't you . . . what? . . ."

Noise of Mr. Grotti twisting his body into new position on bed bounced his wife into a panic of abstraction. A horde of outraged warnings torn from headlines of daily newspapers swept through her mind. She lost all peripheral vision. Her memory was shaking like a suitcase of old shoes. She waited, tensed for the impact of a shoe tossed from the livingroom.

"Kill! Kill! Kill!" the clock said. "Kill! Kill! Kill!"

Mrs. Grotti was irritated by wing lines of sweat that flitted down her back like a swarm of green flies. She unconsciously tightened her womb grip around her knees, her nightgown blotting up the sweat. She could hear her own heart beat and Mr. Grotti's muffled breathing.

"Don't you remember them, Dominic?" she unexpectedly picked up where she'd left off. "Come on, you must . . . we all went out together on New Year's Eve to that splashy party at the Victor Club. Your business associates were all there, decked out to kill, I must say, in fashionable tuxedos and they wore the same color turtleneck sweaters. Hm-m-m, I forgot what color that was?"

She desired signals from her husband but Mr. Grotti said nothing. He remained as still as the burglar, whose nose had silently started to run. His body sore and itchy, the burglar had to concentrate on breathing through his mouth and not yawning.

"What's the matter with you, Dominic... are you sick, or completely not interested?" Mrs. Grotti pleaded in a shaky, tremulous voice. She drew in a deep breath to calm herself down, and stretched her numb fingers. "Don't you even remember how long we did it after we came home that night. It felt great. You, Jeannie, and I had gotten so pleasantly drunk on that kid drink, rum and coca-cola...

"As for Steve, you know, Jeannie's present husband, he was in some other world. If you didn't notice, he's a lot younger than Jeannie. I think he takes drugs... look at how many times he went to the men's room or stepped outside for a breath of fresh air. He always came back to the table dizzy-eyed and confused. You couldn't make heads or tails of what he was mumbling about, and I never once saw him with a drink in his hand...."

The bed springs squeaking again interrupted Mrs. Grotti's home movies of the past. She peeked at her husband. Mr. Grotti was doing push-ups. His voice went from soft to loud to massively angry.

"Yes, I seem to recall both of them, now I want you to shutup forever about how a man's body performs in bed. Or Else. GODDAMIT!!!" Mr. Grotti's arms had suddenly locked at the peak of his last push-up. He was stuck there until his legs and arms would collapse in a heap like dirty laundry.

"Jesus Christ, take an eyeful of me now. What a mess!... Mary, would you please let out what those busybodies said about me."

"Yes, Dominic, I was just getting to that," she announced dramatically and scratched the soft folds of her stomach. "I was waiting on line, minding my own business. Bohack's was crowded. There were six or seven people in front of me. And the two old ladies complaining quietly about their arthritic feet and pains in their shoulders. Then they both threw hide 'n seek glances back at me. And one of them—she was wrapped up in a gray check overcoat and a plain black kerchief—started rattling to her friend in a loud whisper so half the store could hear that your insurance business isn't all it's collected to be. She also remarked that the men who work for you look more like gangsters than insurance salesmen. 'Now what good is that type of person for a business?' she finally asked, her arms outstretched, practically shouting. The other old hag, who was carrying her groceries in a green plastic shopping bag, smiled, looked directly at me over the shoulder of her blabbermouth friend, and blared out, 'That depends on what kind of insurance you're selling.' Let me tell you, Dominic, I was almost out of my mind with rage. I yearned so bad to scratch that smirking witch's eyes out with my long, manicured nails. But I have too much respect for myself and didn't want to start a scene. Later on I made up my mind that those two old ladies must be crazy . . . now I'm not so sure."

Mrs. Grotti started to bite each one of her knuckles.

There was a long silence that seemed even longer than twenty seconds to the rigid burglar. His ears were erect for the last solemn moments, and his mind was breaking up into small, useless armed camps. A fiery sinking sensation in the pit of his stomach. He was afraid to move backwards, he couldn't remember if a coffee table was behind him or not. He heard the clock ticking on the dresser in the bedroom. His damp shirt stuck to his back. His punctured arms hung limply at his sides, fingers barely touching the seams of his pants.

Mr. Grotti collapsed on the bed, his face in the pillow, a pile of dirty laundry. "What the hell does she think she's doing to me?" he wondered to himself. "Why it's all a bunch of happy horseshit."

He got up to his knees and slapped his wife hard on the side of her head.

"You get this straight, woman," he yelled. "The men who work for me are my friends and don't you ever call them gangsters again."

Mr. Grotti's face and neck were damp. He closed his eyes and with an effort overcame a sudden sickness.

"So you want to know where I get my money, do you!" The words rose hoarsely from somewhere deep down inside his chest.

"All right, I'll tell you, if it'll make you happy . . . I run the numbers racket in this neighborhood and I squeeze protection from the stores on 1st and 2nd Avenues from 79th Street to 92nd Street."

Mrs. Grotti began to cry into both of her hands.

Mr. Grotti wiped his mouth with the back of his hand and scratched his nose. He reached over and tried to take his wife's hands away from her face.

"Leave me alone!" Her words snapped out, then dying in the breathless air.

"What's the matter with you?" Mr. Grotti gently stabbed a finger into her ribs. "You wanted to know, so now you know. And there's nothing you can do about it. Either you accept it, or . . . I don't know what."

The burglar touched the back of his neck. It felt like a target on a pistol range, bull's eye between his shoulder blades. And he also couldn't get it out of his head that somehow his shoelaces had been tied together.

Mrs. Grotti stopped crying and listened to sounds of the ocean in the noise of passing cars. She was afraid of the warm heavy darkness. It made her expect a thunderstorm. "I accept it," she said. All her energy blown away, she seemed to sag, become fatter with her neck lost between her shoulders. She really didn't know what she was saying: "But Dominic, aren't you afraid you might get arrested, or even worse, someone might kill you?"

Mr. Grotti felt depressed and unbelievably tired. He gazed spellbound at his wife's dark shoulder length hair. His broad, sweaty face, alternately hot and cold, was a picture of overwhelming weariness. He was waiting for the laughing burglar to charge into their room. What agony it would be . . . what effort to turn over and get up, but he knew he'd have to put up a fight.

"If that bastard doesn't have a gun or knife, maybe I can deck him!" Mr. Grotti was trying to psyche himself up. Images of incredible sadism rumbled across the vast night background of his brain.

"I don't have to be afraid of anything," he told his wife.

"You've been watching too many movies on t.v."

"But what about me and the kids?" She was holding back the pressure of self-pity behind her watery eyes and in her throat. "What if some thief, who knows about you, breaks into the house when you're not here."

Instinctively the burglar took two steps backwards, squatted down close to the rug and melted into the darkness like a piece of caramel candy. He was filled with a great unrest and crazy desires, but he'd wait until he was sure they were asleep before he got the hell out of there.

It took Mr. Grotti a long time to answer his apprehensive wife. He rolled his eyes and pressed both hands against his chest. For an instant he thought that his head was packed in ice. His heart might shake out of his body. He let himself fall back to the pillow. He had opened a trapdoor in his mind and suddenly everything headed for the exit.

Mr. Grotti spread out his arms, put one around his wife's back, and said:

"You don't have to worry about that, Mary. Didn't I just tell you I run a protection racket. One of the boys checks by the house at least six or seven times a day."

The burglar glanced nervously out the front window.

"And I don't keep any money in the house," continued Mr. Grotti, all of a sudden very pleased with the sound of his own strong voice. "I keep it in the bank or in my office safe. If a thief wanted to rob our apartment he'd have to rent a truck and sell the stuff to a fence, and I know all the fences. I'd have that guy wiped out so fast people would start calling me the invisible man."

Mr. Grotti pulled his wife down and kissed her long and hard. He relaxed, his head resting on the palms of his hands. He spoke to the ceiling:

"You know, if I were a thief working this neighborhood, I'd rob the Gaggiano's house in a hurry."

"Huh! Who's that?" Mrs. Grotti took the words out of the burglar's wide open mouth.

"Nick and Helen. You know, they live on the fifth floor next door, and they're thinking about buying a house on Long Island. The buzzer system in their building has been broken now for two months. A guy could walk in there, go up to the roof, and get on Nick's fire escape as simple as you please. Of course Nick locks his kitchen window and has an iron gate on it too, but the jackass leaves the small bathroom window wide open. He's a fresh air nut, he'll tell you. What a clown! All any dumb crook really needs is a wooden plank as a bridge to crawl from the fire escape into the window. . . .

"And you know what else that fat jerk Nick likes to do?" Mr. Grotti paused to knock some hair off his greasy forehead before he answered his own question. "He keeps a lot of money around the house just in case he needs it for something right away. He tells you about a Saturday night a few years back when he could've bought an almost brand-new Cadillac for only eight hundred cash. But he didn't have the dough in his pockets or around the house. He's a big man, and smart too! You know where he hides all his money at night? . . . In the breadbox on top of the refrigerator. The first place a good thief would look for it. What a dope!"

Mr. Grotti sat on the edge of the bed. He reached for his robe and stuffed his feet into his half-worn slippers.

The burglar's body quivered a moment, tightened. He opened his knife, drawing it up the side of his pants.

Mr. Grotti turned to his wife.

"Honey, let's go into the kitchen and have a cup of coffee."

"Okay, Dominic," she said. "But should we put a light on first?"

"No," he answered. "It might wake up the kids."

Mr. Grotti held his wife's shaking hand as he led her through the dim sleeping rooms.

After a couple of minutes of remaining perfectly still, the burglar got up, and climbed noiselessly out the front window . . .

At seven a.m. next morning the superintendent of 348 called the police. He had discovered the dead body of a man in the back yard. The man's spine was broken and his head cracked open. His brains were pouring out on the concrete along with his blood. Several feet away from him lay a splintered board of wood. There were also electrical burns across the palms of the dead man's hands.

The police and ambulance sirens woke up Mr. Grotti. He smiled to himself, rubbed his wife's warm breasts, and went back to sleep. . . .

MOTHER OF GOD

The shiny yellow cab turned onto Queens Boulevard and slowly headed towards the 59th Street Bridge. It was a Saturday night in July, ten fifteen pm, hot and sticky like a beach blanket. Other cars whizzed by, sportscars, convertibles and those wide jeeps with inflated wheels. Kids had taken over the roads, going to and from parties, getting high, getting drunk and yelling out windows at the tops of their lungs.

Pete McGowan's shoulders sagged into his chest; his face was puffy and red; his sweaty tee-shirt no longer white. He was an old Irish man, a widower with white hair and arthritis in his hands and hips. His wife had died nearly thirty years ago when their son, Jamie (James Timothy), was six years old. Pete was left with nothing but his cab, a mortgage and his son. He became both mother and father to that boy.

Pete had been watching tv in the livingroom, but he got restless and since he wasn't allowed to drink because of the blood pressure pills he was taking (it had been his favorite way to fall asleep), he decided to take the cab out for a while. At least then he could talk to real people.

Pete had bought his taxi medallion during the war from a fellow Galway man who'd retired. He used it on six cabs; all of them named Deirdre after his wife. And he decorated this cab with pictures of Ireland he had taken on his latest trip back.

He stayed in the right lane with his off-duty sign on. He wanted to talk, but he didn't want to pick up a passenger who was in a great hurry to get into the city. That would only increase his chances of having an accident. The Taxi and Limousine Board had politely suggested to him that he should retire. He tried to shut down all his thoughts and concentrate on the road.

Bridge traffic was light both ways.

Manhattan was full of monstrous lights, unceasing noise and people in a hurry to get somewhere else. Pete was waiting for the green light at 59th Street and Second Avenue when he got his first fare. He had just turned off the off-duty sign; overhead a cablecar was heading for Roosevelt Island.

"Second Street and First Avenue, please."

A not-so-young young man, carrying a walkman and wearing white shorts and a sleeveless black tee-shirt, sat back in the cab.

"Bejesus, it's a hot night out there."

"Yes, it's hot all right."

There was writing on the front of his tee-shirt in dripping purple paint: Balm in Gilead.

Pete couldn't make out the words through the rearview mirror; even if he had he wouldn't have known it was a play or remembered it from the Bible. It was late enough for the traffic going downtown not to be that heavy. Stop and go was the thing Pete hated the most. His blood pressure and arthritis. He saw his passenger put on the walkman. Detestable things, Pete thought. He tried to swallow then ran his tongue over his cracked lips. His throat hurt and he was having a difficult time breathing through his nose. At the next light he would drink some tea from his thermos.

"My son . . . ah . . . me son, he died last week."

The passenger took off his earphones.

"What did you say?"

"My son died last week."

"I'm sorry to hear that."

"He died of AIDS."

"Oh, that's terrible." The passenger replaced his earphones and sank into a corner. He turned up the volume and looked out the window. At the next light, Forty-third Street, Pete drank some tea. He felt better.

Why did his son have to die? It all had happened so fast. Maybe this man in the back seat knew something about it. Maybe he could help Pete comprehend. It was scaring off everyone Pete knew. Only five people from the family had shown up at Jamie's funeral. And ten queer friends. Pete had gone to a parish in Manhattan to bury Jamie; there was a service but no mass.

What was the word newspapers used for these people? "Gay," that was it. In Ireland "gay" had meant a rich young gentleman who took advantage of serving girls who didn't know any better. And hadn't he also read in the papers that a priest had died of AIDS? Did the Church bury its own? Or did they give the priest away to some gay society?

"My son was a homosexual. I saw him one night outside one of those bars over by the docks. There were dozens of men. And my boy was rubbing himself against a motorcycle."

The passenger took off his walkman.

"Are you talking to me?"

Pete turned his whole body around and nodded, his eyes were wet.

"Driver, what the hell are you doing? Are you insane or what? Turn around and keep your eyes on the road."

Pete turned around and stared at the white Cadillac in front of him; its license plate read: WILD ONE. The rest of the ride downtown was uneventful. The man got out at his destination, right in front of a liquor store; he gave Pete a seventy-five-cent tip.

The cab turned up First Avenue; Pete smelled baking bread from a storefront bakery. It was both delicious and oppressive in the heat. At Fifth Street a shinyfaced man in a white shortsleeve shirt was waving furiously; his very pregnant wife was leaning against a car.

Pete pulled over.

"Señor, Bellevue Hospital fast, please. My wife she will now have a baby."

He helped his wife into the cab with elaborate care. Pete knew right away that the young guy didn't have the slightest idea what to do in an emergency. In all the years Pete had been driving a cab no one had given birth to a baby in his back seat, but there had been quite a few close calls, weren't there, Deirdre. Pete smiled, and before he took his foot from the brake to the gas pedal, he turned around and said:

"This ride's on me."

He stepped on the gas and put on the off-duty sign.

"Thank you, Señor, thank you much."

The expectant mother nodded recognition of the favor then closed her eyes. Her face exploded sweat and her maternity shift was sticking to her stomach and breasts. Pete could smell her fear and nervous exhaustion. He asked:

"Is this your first one?"

The man answered:

"Si, señor. My name is Victor Rivera and my wife's name is Wanda."

"A neighbor of mine has a daughter named Wanda, but she's Polish."

That Wanda was twenty-seven, overweight and a social worker; she still lived with her parents five houses down from Pete's. All the houses on the block were built at the same time, red brick and connected.

Wanda had known Jamie for a long time; every once in a while they had gone out together to the movies. She called him J.T. She must have known that he was a homosexual but she hadn't said a word to Pete. Maybe he should talk to her about what he was feeling, but she didn't go to Jamie's funeral and neither did her parents. She had mumbled something about how truly sorry she was when she passed the house the day after the funeral on her way to work. Pete had been polishing his cab.

This Wanda moaned in the back seat. Pete glanced at his rearview mirror. The pain of a contraction was visible on her face. In a way he didn't mind if she had her baby; Deirdre would be proud and maybe get its picture in the papers. But what if a reporter asked Pete about his family? Could they find out how Jamie died? Sure they could. But did Pete care anymore whether people found out? He wasn't sure if he wanted to talk about it.

The cab arrived at Bellevue Emergency without any mishap. Victor rushed in to get help. Pete got out from behind the wheel and opened the other back door. Sitting next to Wanda, he took her hand and tried to smile but couldn't manage it. Instead he stroked it and said soothingly:

"Ah, bejesus, it'll be all right. Your husband will bring the doctor. Everything will turn out for the best. You'll have a fine healthy baby, and he'll grow up to be big and strong. I'll remember him in my prayers."

He touched her stomach; it tightened and jumped with a contraction. He took his hand away. He thought, "I'll pray it doesn't grow up to be like my Jamie."

He told Wanda:

"Maybe your son will grow up to be a doctor or a policeman."

Victor arrived with a wheelchair and a nurse.

"Calm down, Mr. Rivera, we'll get her upstairs in a jiffy."

They both helped Wanda into the wheelchair. Victor pushed it towards the Emergency Room. He yelled over his shoulder, "Thank you, señor, for all you do."

Pete half smiled; he got out of the back seat and stood there with his hands in his pockets, staring at the Emergency Room's swinging doors. Maybe he should follow them in and wait to see what happens. He could stay with Victor and try to calm him down. But he remembered they don't deliver babies they way they did when Jamie was born. Nowadays fathers go into the delivery room with the doctors and nurses.

Pete felt that he wouldn't like to see all that blood and slime and the umbilical cord. If he had helped deliver Jamie, would it have made any difference in the end? He shrugged his shoulders; he was dying for a drink.

He climbed into his cab and drank some tea. He drove slowly out of the hospital complex; he turned off the off-duty sign. He blamed himself for Jamie's death. He prayed:

"Mother of God, pray for us sinners now and at the hour of our death. Amen."

A sandyhaired, irishlooking kid was leaning against a lamppost on Twenty-eighth Street, his right arm in a sling, one eye bandaged. He had just walked out of Emergency without paying or giving his right name; he had used Kevin O'Rourke, an ex-friend of his from Bayside, and given O'Rourke's correct address. The kid's real name was Ammon Connelly. He didn't like his first name; he'd rather be called Kool Gone Breeze. K.G.B. was his tag. As for his last name, his father could take it back anytime and shove it up his ass until it came out his donkey ears.

"You want a cab, me lad?" Pete leaned over and asked.

"Yeah," the kid frowned; he didn't like Irish accents. "And I'm going to Queens."

"Which part?"

"Woodside." He paused and put his free hand into pocket of his dungaree shorts. "And I only have four dollars."

"That's all I'll charge you, no matter what the meter says. I live in Queens and I'm heading home."

Ammon stretched himself out in the back seat. He was a very white, muscular eighteen-year-old kid with a hint of emerging beer belly. He lived at home with his parents and two younger sisters he thought were stone-cold bitches. He had dropped out of high school at the end of his second year, was rejected by the Army, used drugs if he could get them, and whenever he worked, he worked as a plumber's helper.

The cab breezed towards the 59th Street Bridge; traffic wouldn't get congested until 53rd Street, then it would be slow all the way. Ammon looked around inside the cab.

"Nice cab you got here, Pops."

"It's me own. I named it Deirdre after my late wife."

Pete wondered whether he should tell this kid about Jamie. Instead he asked:

"What kind of work do you do?"

"Plumbing."

"Well it looks like you won't be doing much of that for a while."

"Yeah, I know," Ammon replied and to himself he added: "You dumb old mick."

"You know, a woman nearly had a baby in the back seat just before you."

Ammon looked for wet spots. None. Pete continued:

"I dropped her and her husband off at the Emergency Room. Victor and Wanda Rivera. A nice young couple but he was very nervous. I almost stayed there to calm him down."

Ammon understood why the old fart was only charging him only four dollars to Woodside. He wanted someone to talk to. Traffic had slowed down but it continued to move. Ammon didn't care, all his Saturday night fighting had been knocked out of him. All he wanted was a quart of beer.

Why couldn't Jamie have been more like this boy, Pete thought. A little trouble but nothing serious. A young lad was expected to sow his wild oats. Get drunk and throw a few punches. Jamie had been so serious, always studying or reading in his room. At one time he had wanted to be a priest.

Pete realized he had been staring at the kid through the rearview mirror. He looked ahead, he was driving up the ramp onto the bridge. The urge to talk seriously to this kid was getting stronger. Young people were supposed to be more understanding. But his Jamie hadn't been. After sixteen he always made a point of talking down to Pete, his own father. Pete never would have done that to his father.

"So if you don't mind me asking, how did you hurt yourself?"

"In a fight."

"Where?"

"At a bar. Some guy put his hand on my ass and I punched him in the mouth. He got up and we took it outside. As we went through the door he sly-rapped me." Ammon pointed to his bandaged eye. "The guy stomped on my arm while I was down. He went back inside and they locked the door. I wanted to kill that cocksucker so bad. Then the cops came and brought me to Bellevue."

Ammon sat up straight with rage then leaned towards Pete's shoulder.

"The guy was a fucking faggot. I hate the sight of them. If I had my way they'd all be dead. Burn their balls off. All they do is give people diseases."

Ammon sat back in his seat, looking relieved all of a sudden as if he had jerked off. Outside the gray motionless sky looked wasted. Pete didn't know what to say. He wanted his Jamie back, like when Jamie was six years old and Pete had held his hand while the priest said the last prayers at Deirdre's grave.

"Holy Mary, Mother of God, pray for us sinners, now and at the hour of our death. Amen."

Ammon sat up again.

"Let me off at the next corner, willya."

"Sure," Pete said. "And you don't have to pay me. Go buy yourself a beer."

"Thanks, Pop."

Ammon slammed the door behind him and walked off. In another ten minutes Pete was parked in his driveway. He shut off the lights and the engine. He sat there in the dark with his mind in reverse, his shoulders sagging into his chest. Finally he touched the dashboard and said:

"Deirdre, our son died last week. He died of AIDS."

Johnny Stanton

He took a deep breath.
"Where did I go wrong?"
Then it all spilled out like oil. . . .

MODERN LOVE

"Broadway, how long have we been going together?"

Broadway looked up from her book; she was stretched out on the bed. No clothes on. Surrounded by books. Her evenly tanned body contrasted sharply with her white bikini skin.

"Let me think for a minute." She nonchalantly groomed her pubic hairs with frost pink fingernails. "Six and one is seven carry the two. Zero minus one to the ninth power, which is, as I'm sure you know, Stanton, a very mystical number to the Gnostics."

"Come on, Broadway, I'm not playing around. I'm just asking a civilized question."

"I can see that, you still have your clothes on."

Stanton took off his green t-shirt and maroon and white stenciled shorts. He pushed some library books off the bed.

"What are you reading about now, Broadway?"

He picked up a book and answered his own question:

"*Milton: The Mind of a Puritan.*" He screwed up his face. "What are you, out of your mind?"

She nodded affirmative several times. Her hair spiked orange like a rusty fence.

He put down the book and lay next to her. He put his hands behind his neck, his knees in the air, and did fifty situps as quickly and as hard as possible. Broadway tossed her book on the floor; she sensed something was about to happen and she didn't want control.

It was a hot Sunday afternoon in her small air-conditioned apartment. Stanton had spent the night; they had made love last night and this morning, then a break for breakfast, a giant meal. Stanton was an early riser like Milton. Thank God that was the only bad habit he shared with the Great Puritan. Broadway used to think breakfast was just a big cup of coffee. But with all the sex surrounding it, you definitely needed something to eat.

And now more sex.

Time passed excitedly.

"Why do you always pop out?" Broadway got a kick out of this ritual question because Stanton hadn't figured out an automatic answer yet. He just squirmed and pretended to be annoyed.

"If you hadn't told me to come, I'd still be inside you." He changed his voice to imitation delta blues singer. "Baby, you know I always give you what you want. I've been put on this earth just to please you."

"Bullshit. We please each other, Stan. I wanted to feel you come inside me because I knew that would make me come again."

"For the eighty-eighth time," he bragged in her ear.

She suddenly jumped to her knees and punched him in the stomach as hard as she could. "Sexist white trash."

He laughed in her face.

"Sorry, Broadway, I'm just too hard for you."

So far none of her stomach shots had made him even wince. Surprise didn't seem to matter.

"Why did you ask me before how long we've been going together?"

"Oh, nothing important," he shrugged his shoulders. "I just wanted to know."

"Stanton," she shook her finger, "don't be a vagina."

"I'm not, honest I'm not."

They lay on the bed listening to the air conditioner.

"I'm cold," Broadway rattled her teeth. "Put a sheet over me, honey, please."

Stanton hesitated. He had always suspected that her teeth rattling was a trick she could perform on command, like making your tongue touch your nose. But what could he do . . . make an issue out of it? That would be absurd. So he got up with a growl and covered her with a sheet.

They had been going together two and a half years. He was no longer married, and he hadn't seen either one of his exes in over a year. He was living with a friend, an illegal alien, in Brooklyn by the Williamsburg Bridge, surrounded by Puerto Ricans, Italians and chain-smoking Russians.

"Broadway, let's get married."

Broadway's eyebrows bounced like rubberbands.

"That's not the way you're supposed to ask."

"What do you mean, not the way I'm supposed to ask?"

Broadway sat up with the sheet draped around her shoulders.

"You know what I mean!"

Stanton sighed and dropped to his knees at the altar of her bed. Two knees on one book. He clasped his hands together and prayed:

"Holy Virgin Broadway, I want to keep my eucharistic cock inside you forever. So please marry me."

She was pleased; she had given the idea of marriage a lot of rumination over the years. She had gone from never wanting to get married—she hated the idea of sharing any values with her mother—to sincere doubts on the viability of the institution, to clearheaded acceptance if it was in the cards. She thought marriage was like a swimming pool filled with cold water and too much chlorine. But what were you going to do on a hot day? The ocean was too far away and rough, and the bathtub was too small.

"Yes. Yes. Yes," she quoted Molly Bloom.

Stanton caught the literary reference. He liked it very much. From under his knees he picked up a hardcover copy of Milton's complete works and handed it to Broadway. He pointed to his stomach.

"You can hit me with it as hard as you want."

She laughed in his face and kissed him all over.

"No regrets?"

"No regrets."

She slammed his stomach with Milton. A red welt the size of the book instantly appeared. Stanton took a quick deep breath: grind your teeth, hide the pain. A makeshift smile.

"Why the fuck are you reading Milton?"

"He's the second greatest poet in the English language and he's going to be the hero of my next performance poem, *Penis Envy*. I want to take the most masculine writer I know and prove that underneath he was really a faggot. I almost decided on Melville but Milton was a bigger prick. Listen to this."

She thumbed through her weapon. She pointed furiously:

"From Book IV of *Paradise Lost*. He's talking about Adam and Eve.

> 'The image of their glorious Maker shone,
> Truth, wisdom, sanctitude severe and pure—
> Severe, but in true filial freedom placed,
> Whence true authority in men: though both
> Not equal, as their sex not equal seemed;
> For contemplation he and valour formed,
> For softness she and sweet attractive grace;
> He for God only, she for God in him.'"

"It boggles the mind." Stanton shook his head reflectively. "Broadway, if you took the telescope on top of Mount Wilson and put it inside the telescope on top of Mount Palomar, you still wouldn't be able to see my interest in Milton. I think most of your ideas for poems suck . . . suck moose cock as a matter of fact. But you're a fucking genius and your performances are totally great. One of these days I want you to perform one of my stories. Maybe when my first book comes out. You know that's the only reason I want to marry you."

Broadway threw open her legs, pointed in between and drawled: "That and my vagina."

* * * * *

"Come on, get your ass out of bed, honey, please."

Stanton rolled over; his head hurt, and Broadway must have poured cotton down his throat while he was asleep. Last night. Oh God. A bachelor party at his age was pretty stupid stuff. Who was that guy he had thrown over the table? A tremendous effort of Will pried his eyes open. *Paradise Lust?* He wondered if writers had felt like this is the seventeenth century. Probably not.

"Broadway, what was the name of that character in *Parade's End* who loved the seventeenth century?"

"Tietjens. Christopher Tietjens."

"He was an ass."

"No he wasn't."

"Yes he was."

"No he wasn't." Broadway was standing at the bottom of the bed with her hands on her hips. The color of her hair was growing brown; she had just taken curlers out, something she hadn't used since she was fourteen. Last night she'd been glad Stanton was too drunk to notice. "Now that that literary argument is settled, Stan, get your ass out of bed. We have to go to my mother's for brunch."

"Fuck you, you cunt, and fuck your mother's cunt too."

"Stanton, you promised not to use that word. If I told you once I told you a thousand times, political women got pissed off at me when I used it in my poems, so I don't use it anymore. Remember all that shit I got when I performed my poem *If I Only Had a Cunt*?"

Stanton grinned like a shiteater, remembering a furious circle of shouting women, and himself thinking he might have to rescue Broadway. A good thing he had gone out for a beer.

Broadway pressed her hands further into her hips. She could see the sarcastic images inside Stanton's head. He was very easy to read. She continued with increasing accusation:

"And besides, what kind of pussy would I look like to my radical lesbian friends if I let my intended use a four-letter word I didn't allow myself to use anymore?"

"A vaginahead."

Broadway filled up a pitcher of cold water and threw it all over him. Then she ran out of the apartment. Stanton dripped out of bed. He put on his glasses and investigated his image in the mirror over the sink.

"Yuck!" He splashed cold water on his wet face and looked again. "Double yuck! Well, at least I only got drunk last night and not completely fucked up. That was an achievement."

He went into the bathroom and took a crap. He wiped himself quickly, the smell was unbearable. He turned on a small blue fan that was sitting on top of the refrigerator and pointed it towards the bathroom.

"Mrs. Trezbinski, I want to marry your daughter. As if you fucking care. As if I ever fucking met you before. Your daughter hates your guts and thinks you're a fascist. So why this big deal? I could never figure out families. It's the female hand-me-down knowledge that blows me away."

A knock on the door.

"If that's you, Broadway, you better have the *Times*, donuts and some coffee. And then maybe I'll marry you."

"It's me . . . Saint, and you can't marry me. I'm going to be a witness."

Stanton fought down the urge to fling open the door and declare himself to be Jehovah revisited. He sniffed the air and was too embarrassed to open the door even a crack. He wasn't always such a chicken shit; he remembered taking acid and getting drunk in college once, then waking up in his own vomit and rolling in it in front of a tittering audience of college girls sitting on a couch in someone's large livingroom. The acid had told him it was an important thing to do.

"Broadway isn't here, Saint, and I'm not dressed. Come back later."

"Okay."

For the life of him, Stanton couldn't figure Saint out. First of all, that wasn't her real name. Stanton didn't know what it was. Broadway's real name was Anna Trezbinski. All the women Broadway knew had different names. It was like being introduced to a group of Black Muslims, some of whom you knew in high school: it was very confusing.

He had never met a woman friend of Broadway's that was as shy as Saint, and she was an actress and a very good one. She was short, not too thin, pretty in a boyish sort of way, but you definitely got the idea that she was trying to hide her body . . . up to a point. Stanton could tell that she was proud of her legs; she roller skated everywhere. She wore cut-up jeans, but always left the impression that the rips had just happened.

Maybe she thought her tits were too small. Maybe she didn't like boys. Maybe she didn't like girls. Maybe her parents didn't like her. Who knows? Who the fuck cares? Just thinking about it gave Stanton another headache on top of the monumental one he already had.

The door banged open.

"For Chrissakes, Stan, get dressed."

"Yes dear," he sighed.

Stanton smelled the coffee, saw the *Times* and imagined the donuts in the greasy brown bag.

"Saint knocked on the door."

"Yeah . . . so?"

"I wouldn't let her in no matter how much she begged for my body."

"She wouldn't sleep with you, she likes me better. She's my friend."

"But what if you get sick and die like you're always telling me you might. Could I make a play for her then?"

"She doesn't like baseball."

"But I'm a switch hitter," Stanton smirked.

Broadway thought she ought to punch him in the stomach for making such a lousy joke—he's hung over, he wouldn't be expecting it—but instead she made a face.

"What stinks?"

A sheepish grin. "Decaying parts of my body," Stanton replied.

She handed him the container of coffee, took a jelly donut out of the bag and put it near his mouth.

He took a big bite a slugged his coffee.

"I juu shoe."

"What are you babbling about?" Broadway held her nose and closed the bathroom door.

"I love you, Broadway," Stanton giggled. "I really do,"

Broadway's body melted into her polished green eyes; she looked at her watch.

"Let's have a quickie before brunch."

Stanton's dick saluted her. . . .

* * * * *

"Come in, come in." Mrs. Trezbinski smiled in a faintly serious way. "Anna, you and yours will always be welcome in my home."

She was not at all what Stanton expected. He had expected a short fat Polack woman who looked like Jack Kerouac's mother. Instead, Mrs. Trezbinski was a thin-hipped woman in her early fifties, wearing two strands of pearls around her neck. She had polished green eyes like Broadway and her brown hair was held in place by lots of spray. She welcomed Stanton on the lips, her mouth hanging loose like a ribbon.

Her apartment was in a building with a carefully tended garden in back. She lived in four rooms crowded with fragile, antique furniture, each piece beautiful to look at by itself, but massed together too much for the eye to take in. Stanton remembered the livingroom of his childhood; he hadn't been allowed to play in there because of the furniture, which was covered in the summer with sheets.

A man in an apron popped out of the kitchen. He was bald, middle-aged, sweaty, with a red face . . . Eastern European. He wasn't tall but he gave the appearance of being fairly healthy and strong. A survivor. His eyes were his most striking feature, they were like plums dropped into cold water.

"Anna," Mrs. Trezbinski stuck out her chest. "You're not the only one with a literary man in your house."

The inner flame of Broadway's thoughts burned the hell out of her tongue. "I am a literary woman," she muttered to herself, but with her mother she kept to the point.

"Please introduce us."

"Konstanty, this is my daughter, Anna, and her fiance."

Stanton was introduced to the chef.

"I am much pleased to make your acquaintance." Konstanty bowed.

To Stanton he sounded like an old pagan chief from long ago Treasure Island movies.

"When did you come to the United States?" Broadway asked.

"Six months ago. I try now to get my father's play translated and published in English."

"Who was your father?"

"Konstanty Ildefons Galczynski."

"That name sounds familiar." Broadway stood motionless as an exclamation point. "Is your father . . . the Green Goose?"

"Don't you mean the Green Hornet, Broadway?" Stanton sniggered out of the side of his mouth.

Broadway's right hand went stiff as a knife.

"Grow up, Stanton, and stop showing how provincial you are, especially since you're not."

Stanton looked at Mrs. Trezbinski as if to say, that's some daughter you got there. Mrs. Trezbinski smiled and winked like a frog.

"I am also researching a play about the partitions of Poland in the late eighteenth century."

"How boring," Stanton thought provincially. Since Mr. Galczynski was only interested in Broadway for the moment, Stanton decided to trade wits with the not so old lady. And keep one ear open to Broadway's remarks. Jealousy can pop up anywhere, and even if he felt ashamed of himself for feeling this way . . . he felt what he felt and he ought to know everything.

"So, Mrs. Trezbinski, I hear you don't like Jews."

Dead silence. Broadway's eyes flamed on. Mr. Galczynski stared down at his shoes. They were black, well polished but worn out along the edges. He put his hand on Broadway's shoulder as she was about to pummel Stanton's stomach with both fists.

"Dinner it is almost ready," he said, his voice a bit squeaky. "Regina, why you not serve drinks to everyone."

He went into the kitchen with the formal grace of a butler, followed by Mrs. Trezbinski who said over her shoulder:

"All we have are margaritas."

Stanton puzzled a frown. Was Mrs. Trezbinski a Mexican Pole? He thought better of asking Broadway about her heritage. He took off his glasses and rubbed his bloodshot eyes.

When Mrs. Trezbinski was finally out of the room, Broadway exploded:

"You fucking jerk. Why did you want to go and say that?"

His mouth dropped open like a post office; he spread out his penitent arms. Broadway stepped away from him and came back with all her might; she punched him in the stomach.

"I'm sorry," he said.

Broadway walked back and forth over the knots in her stomach.

"Listen, honey," she finally spoke. "We want to get married . . . right?"

"Right." Stanton's shoulders drooped below his chest.

"I haven't got along with my mother for a very long time. And now I want to. For whatever reason. Okay. So you have to help me. I expect that from you. And *you* should want to do that for me."

Stanton for the first time in his life wanted to be like that; the realization rushed through his body like a drug and he straightened himself up proud and tall. A new type of hero. He flashed back to what his marriages were all about and why he had failed at them so miserably. He wouldn't act that way again. Athletic sex wasn't enough. He dug in his heels. No, he was determined not to be like that other Stanton again.

"I got your back, Broadway, and you've got mine." He held her hands. "Back to back we challenge the world. We'll take on any couple in the house. A tag team match. I've never done that with a woman before or for that manner a man. I've always been a loner inside myself. But this is different. It's much too important. Let's try to make it fun and love each other for the rest of our lives."

The promptings of their dreams, incoherent shadows and many lyrical associations passed between them in this livingroom of remembered childhood. Something trembled in the air. The next few seconds softened into desire that melted their faces and punctured their hearts.

"I juu shoe," Stanton beamed, then he formed a ring with his forefinger and thumb and drew it over Broadway's right hand. He held her by the wrists and pulled her close. Outside, the empty Sunday city streets didn't move.

He whispered:

"Let's eat."

* * * * *

After a Mexican-style brunch, everyone relaxed in the livingroom with a pitcher of chilled margaritas. The air conditioner hummed perfectly.

"Mrs. Trezbinski," Stanton was the first to speak. "I'd like to apologize for that impertinent remark before."

"You are instantly forgiven." Her eyes drifted to her daughter. "Anna, I don't think that way anymore." She blushed and her eyes darted back to Stanton. "And please call me Regina from now on." She was sitting next to him on a red velvet couch with a polished oak frame. Her shoes had been left under the round dining room table; her feet were tucked under her derriere. Her light blue dress had slipped up above her knees and Stanton could view at his leisure the creamy insides of her thighs. He already noticed how tight and well defined her muscles were, especially her calves.

"And please call me Stanislaus, Regina."

"It should be Stan the louse instead," Broadway quipped.

"And call me Konstanty." The chef had discarded his apron. He was wearing a shortsleeve white shirt and lime green bermuda shorts. His legs were typically communist and therefore not on anybody's sightseeing agenda.

"And call me Broadway, except you of course, mother."

"Broadway, that's it," Konstanty almost ejected himself from his overstuffed armchair. Broadway was sitting in a similar armchair. A lamp table separated them. Some magazines were stacked on a shelf underneath. Konstanty grinned delightedly, the beams of his face spreading out into self-satisfaction, like a first time guest on a quiz show who's figured out all the answers. He savored every word.

"I read the *Village Voice* from front page to back. I used to read it in Poland whenever I could." He shook his head, remembering the distance. "Not very often. I can only follow the book reviews and the theater section. The rest is bureaucratic gibberish to me. Last month I read an article in the performance section that I understood. The first one. It was about you. The famous performance poet, Broadway. But the article never mentioned your mother. Otherwise I would have known right away it was you."

Broadway's face turned a shade of brownish pink; she lowered her green eyes and said:

"Thank you, Konstanty. Thank you very much." She pointed to the couch. "Stanton wrote that piece. It was the best thing he ever wrote. No, I'm only kidding. He's a fabulous story writer. And he writes travel articles about places he's never been to. He's that good."

She stopped for a moment, took a big margarita drink then put it down on the floor. She wondered why she was talking so fast and bragging about Stan. Something to do with her mother. Stanton puffed up his chest and sipped his sophisticated margarita. Broadway went on:

"We've saved up some money . . . so when we get married, Stan will move in with me. But only his clothes and typewriter. All the rest of his stuff we're going to put into storage." She looked directly at her mother for approval. "And I'm getting a part-time waitress job at a new club that just opened in Chelsea. It's called Lobotomy."

Konstanty's face struggled with the club's name. "What does that mean?" He was hanging on every word Broadway said, including all the gestures and facial moves. He wasn't interested in Stanton because he had already decided that Stanton took too much pleasure in acting like a drunk.

"Lobotomy is an operation where crazy doctors take out your brains and you walk around like a zombie for the rest of your life."

"And a zombie is a person under the control of the State," Stanton interjected; he felt the conversation heating up.

"They have that in Poland," Konstanty kept his eyes fixed on a single point. "But it is only for poets."

Regina raised her glass.

"Let's drink to Konstanty safely here in the United States. Here with me. We have an announcement to make too. We are getting married as soon as it's approved by the Immigration Department."

Broadway drooped slightly forward with a hand on each knee. Stanton whistled softly and scratched his ear; he thought about how the theory of one-upmanship applied in this family: Whoever controlled the dynamics of everyday life always ended up more comfortable than the rest. Broadway was a smart cookie to leave home when she was young.

Stanton motioned to Konstanty to change places. Konstanty

nodded as though he had already thought of it. "That guy's pretty sharp," Stanton said to himself. "He's getting what he wants, and his writing will keep him out of the house. Out of harm's way. And if a mugger doesn't cut his heart out, he'll make the scene. He'll love it."

Stanton said aloud:

"Congratulations. I wish you both the best." He became aware of the moisture on the outside of his glass and in the palms of his hands. He felt obligated to say something more. "Maybe we could have a double ceremony."

Regina stood up and touched Stanton's face. "I would consider that to be one of the nicest moments in my life." Then she raised her glass.

Konstanty stepped up to her, clinked her glass and almost shouted, "Me too."

"Me too," added Stanton as he stood up and clinked their glasses. They all waited for Broadway. Now she was supporting the chair with her back. She struggled forward and picked up her glass from the floor; her lower lip trembled.

"Me too," she whispered and took two giant steps. She clinked everyone's glass at the same time.

"Let's open a bottle of champagne," Konstanty suggested.

* * * * *

Broadway and Stanton, Regina and Konstanty were married in a double ceremony at City Hall. Friday. Clear Indian Summer blue. The witnesses were the same for both couples: Saint and Squireen, a longtime friend of Stanton's, who had struck it rich on the stock market and was now the president of his own trading company. Stanton had given him the nickname after they had seen the movie *The Quiet Man*. Squireen was a very big guy and when Saint stood next to him they looked straight out of the comics, like a Mutt and Jeff routine. He put his arm around her during the ceremony—it covered most of her back—but she slipped gracefully away.

Broadway looked radiant and so did her mother. Broadway had been letting her hair grow and now it reached below her shoulders. For this special occasion it was curled and waved and pumped up grand; its color had become the most natural blonde known to punk downtown hairdressers.

Shew wore a burgundy and white designer dress Saint had bought her as a wedding gift. It clung to Broadway in all the right places. And on top of her tan it was very sexy. Regina had made her own dress, a lovely light green satin thing with lace from her first wedding gown around the neck, waist and sleeves.

Stanton wore a blue pinstripe suit with a vest and a narrow leather tie. The suit had been made by some fag tailor friend of Squireen's so Stanton's muscular build was displayed well. Konstanty had on a brown corduroy suit he had bought on Orchard Street; he had insisted on picking it out and paying for it himself. He wanted a suit he could wear again and again. It made him look like a high school teacher.

After the ceremony they rode in a stretch limousine to a Polish hall that overlooked Second Avenue. It was a swell reception: plenty of good food to eat and powerful drinks to swallow. Regina had arranged and paid for it all except the music. Broadway hired the disk jockey; she had heard great things about him from her friends. He was truly one of a kind. Top of the charts. A scratch master. He automatically beamed into everyone's taste; people boogied and/or danced polkas, whatever felt right.

Every once in a while he could be heard rapping over a record: "I bridge the gap. Wait and see. Only me and my music can set you free. I'll bridge the gap into inner space. Nor even the commies can beat my race."

All his moves and gestures appeared strikingly easy. The records flowed into each other like oil, except once when he leaped into the middle of the dance floor and announced to the world his latest inspired creation.

"It's not rock and roll, not even a polka," he rapped. "A new dance craze that will sweep the nation. It came to me right here in a flash. Watch me slow, watch me fast, my dance is prettier than a baby's ass." He threw his arm into the air like a super star and smiled with all his teeth. As the music started, he shouted: "It's the Disco Soulka."

Everyone stared in boozy amazement. Stanton led the cheers, at the same time thinking he might start calling his penis "John Milton." The dance was so easy, it was learned in a flash. Everybody said it would certainly catch on and spread like crazy. For the rest of the night it was the only dance worth dancing. People who danced congratulated themselves by saying, "You are there," in that old newscaster voice.

Stanton was drinking champagne and orange juice to quench his thirst because he was dancing so hard. This was the first dance he had ever been to where no one refused him. Even in high school where it had been obvious that he was one of the better dancers, sometimes a girl would say, "No thank you." It used to drive him crazy. Now he was in seventh heaven.

But he hardly danced with Broadway—it didn't matter really—he felt very sexy being the center of attention here, and he knew in his secret heart that all his love and sexual attraction was there only for Broadway. He would save the last dance for her. He had brought the record himself. He had already conveyed his choice to the disk jockey, who high-fived wholeheartedly; the song was "Modern Love" by David Bowie.

Meanwhile not everyone was dancing as much as Stanton. Many trips were made downstairs to the spacious bathrooms. People had to pee of course but snorts of cocaine and tokes on joints were being freely offered. Nobody was hassled if they didn't care to indulge and none of the older people complained. A ladies and gentlemen's agreement was formed ad hoc. If the young people kept their drug taking under control downstairs and didn't bring it upstairs, and nobody started a fight, everyone would look the other way.

Of course Stanton and Broadway were offered more drugs

than anyone else. Stanton had been a little surprised when he saw so many women discreetly sniffling their noses before going back upstairs. And there was a long line waiting to get in.

He knew for a fact that the women's room was bigger than the men's. He'd been here once before for some benefit and had drunkenly walked through the wrong swinging door. No one was inside the bathroom except a lesbian poet, wrapped in toilet paper, who was too busy being sick on the floor to care.

Stanton had looked around; he often wondered whether women kept their public restrooms in better shape than men. He himself was very clean and proper, but he knew other men could be quite messy.

It was a clean, well-lighted place with mirrors over each sink. There were twice as many stalls as the men's room. And no graffiti. So based on his empirical research he concluded that women were cleaner than men in thought, word and deed. He hypothesized a reason: women pissed and defecated behind closed doors. There was no penis envy or competition out in the open, which reminded men of their childhood antics of aiming their streams of piss all over the place like submachine guns.

No John Miltons pissing in the wind.

While Stanton danced the night away, Broadway succumbed to the Ladies Room Snorters. She was an easy mark. She had been totally drained by all the last minute nervous preparations for the wedding: she had literally spent days figuring out her personal style of appearances. And last night Saint had kept Broadway up because she was depressed over the absence of any true passion in her life except on stage, which only counted as make-believe. Broadway had made a humongous effort to bring her out of her doldrums. And at dawn Saint had finally fallen asleep in her arms.

Broadway generally didn't do drugs except on special occasions or when she was desperately behind schedule putting together one of her performance poems, especially commissioned ones. She much preferred coffee and guts, and she never used drugs when she actually performed. She had found out very early on that alcohol, uppers, coke or valium only gave her an incredible migraine during her performance, and no amount of aspirin would help. It went away after the show but only if the audience liked her.

It was during her second pee break that Broadway succumbed to temptation; all her old lesbian friends had brought too many grams. Saint made like she disapproved but Broadway didn't care. Upstairs she'd drink champagne, downstairs she'd snort cocaine.

She liked hanging out with lesbians, especially the nasty ones; it made her feel like one of the guys. In that set Broadway was considered tough because she once got into a fight with this really mean bulldyke and laid her low with one quick shot to the stomach.

It had become one of her marital demands that she have a girls' night out. But she thought Stanton had given in too quickly. He'd been acting so different since he had met her mother, almost mysteriously straightforward. No longer a devious bastard or such a smart-ass. She wasn't sure if she liked that. She had gotten used to his old ways. Maybe he could balance them both, and that would be very nice.

At ten o'clock, after most of the older people had said good luck and good night. Regina and Konstanty left for the Waldorf Astoria. Tomorrow afternoon they would leave on their honeymoon: three weeks in Hawaii. Squireen escorted them to the limo, and when he came back, he had a long conversation with Saint. She told him that she thought Broadway was doing too much cocaine.

Squireen said that he would see what he could do. He was a take-charge guy, but this was a delicate situation. After Saint went off to see if Broadway was back upstairs yet, Squireen thought to himself that Broadway had a perfect right to get high whenever the fuck she felt like it. And since there wasn't a ghost of a chance of getting into Saint's panties, he'd forget the whole thing.

He ambled over to the bar and proceeded to get twisted. He knew that after four quick drinks he'd be in a good mood to dance, something he usually didn't to. The music sounded great. From his perch on a stool he watched people doing the Disco Soulka. He bought everyone at the bar a round. He watched Stanton dancing. After another round he called Stanton over for a private lesson. A circle formed around them as Stan demonstrated each step. He showed Squireen how easy it was to lead, then he made Squireen lead him onto the floor. They danced together for five minutes and laughed at all their friends' wise-ass remarks. Once while Squireen was twirling Stanton around, he noticed Saint pushing her way through the gathering crowd and shaking her head "No," directly at him. He winked back at her.

Downstairs the lesbians had taken over the bathroom; nobody could get in without their approval. Of course they let in every woman, so outside their swinging door appearances remained the same. They told anyone who'd listen that they were protecting their turf from transvestites. Broadway listened and laughed. It was all great fun, she thought.

The music upstairs could be heard through the ceiling. Women who came down from the dance floor started to show the hardcore sniffers how to do the Disco Soulka. Its rhythms were infectious, even the most clumsy bulldyke could do it.

Someone exploded with inspiration:

"Let's go upstairs and dance in a circle."

Shouts of approval and sisterhood. "Viva La Revolucion!" They left the ladies room en masse.

Upstairs the place was cooking. Once Squireen was out there dancing, everyone in the place felt the urge. He was definitely a pied piper except to Saint. But she was dancing with him now because he told her he had spoken to Stanton, and he, Stanton, said that he would take care of it himself. It was a delicate situation.

Squireen was about to ask for her phone number—what the fuck, no harm in asking—when the downstairs women arrived and bullied their way into the center of the dance floor.

"A women's dance for the bride," they shouted over and over demonstration style. They formed their circle.

Many of the men turned to Stanton, including Squireen, to find out his response. It was positive. He beamed behind his glasses and nodded "Yes," with his head. But Squireen thought Stanton looked like one of those mechanical toys: a painted bird continually pecking at a mirror.

Stanton didn't know what to think, but he was curious and he didn't want any trouble before he and Broadway danced the last dance. It was too important to him. And he didn't like the picture in his mind of Squireen punching women out, no matter what they did. Maybe the dance would be fun, and besides he had danced one too many Disco Soulkas.

Now the women in the circle were chanting:

"Change the music. Change the music."

"What do you want me to play?" the disk jockey shouted with his hands.

A roar. The reply. In one voice.

"Janis Joplin."

"How about 'A Piece of My Heart'?" He smiled, sweat pouring down from his shaved black head. "I knew for sure someone in this kind of crowd would request it."

The record played. Broadway started to move in the middle of the circle. She was thrilled to be there. She didn't want to be anywhere else. Dancing in her own circle. And within everyone else. Her eyes devoured the women around her, their liberated bodies and passionate faces. Each one danced differently but all together. She understood what she was feeling, but she could hardly express it except in her dance. Milton's puritan face popped into her head. He could never understand this in a million years.

Could Stanton? Janis sang:

"You're out on the street, feeling good..."

Broadway answered in her own heart:

"YES. YES. YES."

Stanton moved closer, attracted by the spectacle of his dancing wife. This celebration of women by women in honor of the bride reminded him of a Jewish wedding. He watched some more, keeping time with his feet. He felt like joining in but understood that he shouldn't.

Squireen was standing next to him, bending over and asking behind his hand:

"Stan, is this some kind of lesbian ritual?"

Stanton answered in a trance:

"I was for that time lifted above earth. / And possess'd joys not promis'd in my birth."

"Come on, Stan, stop acting like a goddam poet, and answer my fucking question."

"What's the question again?"

"Is that circle some kind of lesbian ritual?"

"No, no, not at all. Some of the women in the circle might think so, but they're really celebrating something much older than that. The transfigurational Power of Love and how that love wants to keep everyone alive."

Squireen made a face like he was disgusted, while Janis was repeating:

"Take another little piece of my heart, baby."

Stanton walked towards the disk spinning tables. He signaled the jockey with his eyes then leaned against a speaker, waiting for the song to finish.

When it was over the dee-jay gave Stanton a mike, which he held close to his lips. He said:

"Thank you. Thank you all. Rainmakers. Lifemakers. Songmakers. That was beautiful. A moving occasion. It said more than any of us can understand. And to you, Broadway, all I can give . . . my deepest respect and love for the rest of our lives."

Tears were forming inside his head: a sure sign that he was about to get sentimental. He cleared his throat:

"The next song is the last dance, folks. And if the circle women don't mind, I'd like to dance it with Broadway inside them."

"What's the song?" the circle shouted.

"'Modern Love,'" Stanton stage-whispered. Then he stepped inside the circle into Broadway's arms.

They danced. First Stanton led her through some spins and dips and twirls, but he could tell her mind was still inside her own ritual dance. So he let go of her hands and they each did their own wild steps to the song. Stanton concentrated his desires on Broadway. He imitated her moves, or did their opposite then walked around her to show off.

Broadway was seeing herself as an ancient myth reborn. Which myth? She hadn't the foggiest idea, and it didn't matter. She danced like one possessed.

David Bowie sang:

"Get me to the church on time. . . ."

Broadway lowered her head and shoulders and shook them rhythmically in her dance; Stanton was leaning his upper body back, fingers snapping, and swaying to the music.

David Bowie chanted:

"Modern Love. Modern Love. Modern Love. Modern Love."

Broadway charged into her myth like a bull. Her head smacked into Stanton's stomach. Harder than she ever imagined. Stanton fell over backwards and Broadway fell on top of him. The circle was broken.

She was out like a light. No longer a myth. And Stanton's stomach hurt like hell. Like nothing he had ever felt before. He almost cried. A supreme effort of the Will. *Paradise Lost.*

Why couldn't he have lived in the seventeenth century? As a Cavalier . . . maybe Clarendon. Or an Anglican minister . . . maybe George Herbert. He didn't want to be Milton. Who did he really want to be? *The Compleat Angler*? Yes, that's him. Izaak Walton. "A dead voice seemed to live in a hollow tree."

Squireen carried Broadway to a table. He shook her and sprinkled water on her face. No reaction. He ran to the bar and told the bartender to dial 911. Stanton was helped up from the floor.

He sat on a folding chair with his feet extended and his arms hanging down. People shouted in his ear. He watched the confused outlines of arms and legs rushing over the dance floor. Smoke, thin and blue, drifted up from the basement. Then Squireen put his big hand on Stanton's shoulder and said:

"Come on, Stan, get up. We got to go."

Stanton stood up in the darkness and listened to the silence, harder to hear than the loudest disco. Step by step a circle was formed around him. The beginning of a dream full of unexpected surprises?

* * * * *

Later that night, surrounded by circles of light, Broadway died on the operating table in Bellevue Hospital. From a blood clot in her brain.

"Will the circle be unbroken?
By and by, Lord, by and by."

SATURDAY (EL SÁBADO)

It was Saturday night and I was doing exercises on the corner of 88th Street and 1st Avenue while talking to Pete Moses, an old friend, his wife and three kids. They were stepping out to have pizza pie for dinner and then buy the Sunday newspapers. I hadn't seen them in nearly four months, not since their oldest boy's birthday party. Kevin was eleven years old. Pete was telling me about his new job as program director for teenagers in a community center on the lower east side, and how the increase in salary over his old job— social worker in East Harlem—was helping him pay off his bills. But as usual whenever we get together, our conversation turned to sports, especially hockey. We're both crazy about it. As a matter of fact hockey made us close in the cold boyhood days of our youth. Every highschool fall and winter on Saturday and Sunday Pete used to call for me at ten o'clock and we'd go down to Carl Schultz Park and play rollerskate hockey with anybody who was there, and lots of times we were the only ones. . . . So while Pete and I were gabbing about the old days, and Wanda, his wife, asked the kids to stop running around, a sports car with DPL plates pulled up and parked in front of the fire hydrant where we were standing. Two black diplomats jumped out and glared at each other over the leather roof of the car. This was all they said before they hurried across the street

and tumbled into a fancy bar:
  "Listen, man, fuck you!"
  "Well if that's the way you want to be, man, fuck you too!"

TALES OF SEAN AND SAM

1

My oldest son, Sean, eight years old, and I were heading down 2nd Ave. Going to buy him a pair of sneakers. Summer afternoon, no sun, large gray clouds dropping down from the sky, a sudden storm, thunder, lightning, drops of rain the size of half dollars on the dusty sidewalk. We jumped into a hallway for protection, and the whole time we were there Sean stood perfectly still, his shoulders hunched up, his hands at his side . . . like a dark exclamation point!

2

"Do you know why basketball players can't have babies?" Sean repeats a joke his eleven-year-old friend, Dennis, has just told him.

"Why?" I ask, very intrigued.

"Cause they always dribble before they shoot."

3

A flash flood stormed through the painted desert and killed a whole lot of animals, but the kangaroos weren't hurt too bad because they could jump so high.

4

My youngest son, Sam, five years old, loves to answer the telephone. Early one Saturday morning, when Johanna and I always sleep late, Sam came charging into the bedroom, woke me up, and said: "Daddy... daddy... Karen's mother just died on the phone!"

5

I work in a playground on weekends. Sam wants to go with me every time. One day he found a wrinkled brown paper bag somewhere in the yard. Shoved inside it were paint splattered dungarees, a light gray shirt with thin purple stripes, and all the way at the bottom was a silver .32 caliber pistol with a bone handle. I still have the gun, keep it in my locked desk drawer... no bullets.

6

It's three a.m. "Stormy Monday" is playing on the stereo. I'm the only one up, writing a story about certain sociological events and slow body english. It's very difficult, a prick sleeper, shaking paper, and oh! my aching back in the dust. A nightmare slips into the kids' bedroom. Sean cries out. My sober stomach leaps up from the swivel chair. I zoom into kids' room. Sean tells me he had a bad dream: a giant black duck was chasing him up and down the dirty back stairs of his school. Long rope-like antennas whipped out of its eyes and grabbed at Sean's hands. He woke up frightened and his fingers hurt like he had a cut. Sean asks me if he could go in and sleep with mommy. I say okay and carry him in, give him a kiss, and then go back to my desk. My story comes to me right off the bat. I type it up and call it "Victory at Sea."

THE DAY OUR TURTLE WAS KIDNAPPED

Johanna is getting dinner ready. It's a Wednesday evening. She works quickly with both hands and is humming a medley of songs. The kitchen table is decorated with a vase of flowers and the walls are painted a bright yellow.

I sit at head of table watching Sean and Sam, make sure they don't fool around, holding baseball bat over their heads. I'm high on acid. For the past two months I've dropped a tab every day after work at 3 o'clock.

My heart is jumping around like an egg in boiling water. Someone has kidnapped our turtle today. We live on the ground floor. The turtle was sunbathing in its bowl on front windowsill. The window was open to let in fresh air. Some kid climbed up, grabbed the turtle with two fingers, and went home.

I go into comfortable livingroom and lie down on couch for after-dinner rest of bubbling head and stomach. A halo of magic warmth surrounds me. I read short story by Jack London in between yelling at kids to stop fighting, It's a great story about freedom-fighting lepers in Hawaii.

Outside the rain is walking down 89th Street.

My two-year-old brat, Sam, presses his face against the front window, streaked with his fingerprints, and yells gibberish, or "Hey

Fug!" at anyone who whisks by.

Kindergarten Sean asks me dumb questions about God.

"Who made me, daddy?"

"God made you, Sean."

"Why did he make me, daddy?"

"To turn on, tune in, and fight for the people!"

Sean doesn't get it. His eyes are round and large.

"For chrissakes, Sean, cut it out with these dumbass questions."

"But daddy, the little old lady next door said that God lives above the sky."

"Listen, Sean, the best part of that lady dripped down her father's leg."

Noise of big kids throwing cans at passing cars bang into my ears. A dog barks outside the window.

Sean says, "Daddy, Sam broke two of my crayons today."

"Oh he did, yeah ... hey Sam," I shout. "Come here ... I'm going to cut your peepee off." Sean cracks a bigcity smile. Sam makes funny noises. They both really know I'm just horsing around. My tongue is dry and I feel sticky all over. Scotch tape body, ha ha. Acid sensations sweep down to my toes.

Sam asks me to play tic-tac-toe.

"Fuck off, kid!" I tell Sean. "Go play with your brother. I've got some heavy thinking to do about Man, God, and the Cosmos." Sam fucks off with his brother.

I stare at the ceiling and things begin to lose their heavy outlines. I fixed up and painted this room three months ago, some of it looks pretty good, only had the energy to finish the walls. Steamroller blast, but ceiling's still a dirty yellowish white. Pictures of Staten Island Ferry in circling dawn fog sinks into my mind's eye. The ferryboat is hoarsely blowing blast after blast on its whistle, and from time to time sounds of other whistles come to me out of the mist.

In the distance I hear the screaming bedlam of kids. Sam is the loudest, but now I'm a whirling speck of energy brooding over the world like a gray shadow of infinite mystery. I float above the couch tracing a series of shiny figure eights. My eyes are wide and staring with excitement. My body is trembling violently. I screen my eyes with my hand. The wind is blowing in sudden bursts. Dust everywhere. Then I see large blocks of light, very thick and dense. They hurl themselves at me. . . .

My old lady is shaking me and her voice is shaky asking me why I shout and wave my arms.

"Are you okay?"

"Sure, I never felt better. Cough! Cough! I was just dreaming. It keeps my psyche in shape, you know."

"Do you want a cup of coffee?" Johanna asks.

"Yeah! That'll be great. Then I'll go pull the garbage and do my exercises. I think I'm going to the poetry reading tonight. Do you want to come?"

She points to the kids with her eyes. I let my head fall to one side. It gets stuck there.

"They're upset about the turtle, and I don't think there's anyone to babysit."

Johanna is holding Sean's hand. She takes two deep drags on her cigarette.

"What about Ella?" I suggest.

"She went to play bingo and Dennis and Muffin have gone to Georgia to see a football game tomorrow."

Sam climbs up on the couch, red cheeks smiling, and punches me in the arm to let me know he's upset. We go into the kitchen and Johanna fixes a pot of coffee while I watch evening city news much to Sean and Sam's dismay. They would rather watch Popeye, Superman, or Monster Family. They zip into their room to get some toys. I flash my buddha smile of acid at t.v., but day's events blind me. Bombs in midtown. Skyrocket price of meat. A stranger is beat up, his arms and legs are swollen and his face is all puffed up. Listen, you motherfucker, free all political prisoners sucked into the Belly of the Beast. Thousands of people are roaring out of the frightening city. Back to the small towns and countryside, back to the good old days. Puke shit! But good . . . rain has stopped. The Yankees win and the Mets lose, or is it the Yankees lose and the Mets win? The t.v. is located between the bathroom door and the back window. Johanna's lips brush against my cheek, coffee in front of me. She wants to move into the woods and grass of Pennsylvania. The washing machine is laughing, bloodstains on the toaster. Sam drives his fire truck through the kitchen. "Pee, daddy! Pee, daddy!" He puts out an imaginary fire near the refrigerator. Johanna and I clean up the mess and lecture Sam about using a pot to piss in. I also mention a few things about death and childhood and the ambiguities of sublimation. Sam begins to cry in a high thin voice not his usual frog screech. To cheer him up we all brush our teeth together.

Then I go down the cellar with kids to work out and do the garbage. I'm the superintendent and the acid is still working overtime. I unlock the cellar door. A warm current of air flows past us. The ceiling coming out of the darkness changes colors rapidly. The strong odor of decay . . . makes my skin crawl. I have to hold Sam's hand one step at a time down the steep wooden stairs. Weird images shimmer in my head and collapse. It takes me a few seconds to find the light string.

Sean is yelling for his bike and Sam shouts, "My baska-ball, my baska-ball!"

I pull down the dumbwaiter, it's full to the brim. This really pisses me off. Nothing I hate worse than fat plastic bags of garbage the break on the dumbwaiter, and all sorts of shit fall on my head or into my arms. Sean and Sam are running through sheets and towels on the clothesline. I curse my head off at people who put too much garbage on the clothesline.

The kids look at me sideways like I have a dark hole in my forehead the size of a quarter. Blood streams down my face in four crooked lines, cascades off my chin, and forms a pool between my sneakers. There's no mistake about it . . I'm a dead son of a bitch, Mr. Nixon. But it heats ups the same to me as if I were alive, except I'm stoned out of my head. Oh well, that's life in the big city, kid.

So the motor of furnace starts up on a heart beat. Sam hides his face in his hands. Noise and flame inside boiler always freaks his mind. I tell Sam he's a cretin-idiot. There's nothing to be afraid of as long as you keep your body and your mind in shape for whole life. It's easy enough to do, just remember, never neglect one or the other. Sean nods his head. He agrees with me that Sam is a cretin-idiot, but adds that Sam is also a scaredy-cat. Then I tell Sean about when he was Sam's age and used to put his head between my legs when the boiler started.

"Oh sweat, daddy!" Sean tosses his head from side to side. His body is cut in half and moving in opposite directions. I turn away and stare at light bulb for couple of minutes, landscapes turn on and off. Sean's okay now. The little fucker didn't believe me, thought I was only fooling around.

Meanwhile Sam starts laughing like a cretin-idiot and pushes over two horses and a box. The landlord, a retired seaman, is building his own coffin in the basement. Pretty weird, huh? My mind travels . . . I think about the ancient glory and wisdom of Greece and the Parthenon Bar around the corner. I sure could use a beer and a ball to balance my arithmetic. Heavy acid tells me, "Forget it, bub!" But I don't forget to bring up garbage pails to the street and line them against iron fence so garbagemen will empty them into garbage truck next morning or afternoon. I always like to do the garbage before I go anyplace at night because when I get home it's usually late and I'm too tired drunk or strung out on dope. Sean asks me if we could get another turtle. I tell him that I'll go into Woolworth's tomorrow or the next day and find out how much one costs. The kidnapped turtle's name was Goldberg. He was given to the kids by good friends of ours, Hilton and Pam Obenzinger. Someday I'll tell the world about the previous turtle, Molly, that Sam drowned in boiling hot coffee. . . .

I recite all the Greek I can remember to a group of smiling uniformed men who are standing against the wall where my weights are:

"Δαρείος και Παρυσάτις γίγνον ται παίδες δύο, πρεσβντερος μεν Αρταξέρξης, νεότερος δε Κύρος."*

My defenses of life are slipping into the ground. I'm deathly afraid of these jokers with their waist jackets and bowties. I hurl my knife at them. It bounces off the concrete. Hallucinations? Bogeymen of my childhood . . . I'm a man now with my own family and I shouldn't be scared. I rush at them, my arms flailing, yelling at the top of my lungs.

They disappear like the American Indians. I wonder if the kids think I'm a little nutty. Maybe. I need to calm myself down. I'm spinning around like a black and white disc on a top. The best thing for me to do is work out with my weights.

I start exercising with 100 lb. weights. First, two sets of ten half-squats, then two sets of eight overhead presses. I wipe some sweat off my neck and face with a blue towel. Next exercise, ten bench presses. I make sure not to use my shoulders, back of neck, and feet to help me lift 100 lb. barbell. I lie perfectly still on the bench for several minutes. I think my arms are melting away like ice cubes. So I get up and fool around with the kids for a while. I feel okay. Back to weights, I do twenty side bends with 50 lb. dumbbell, ten on each side. Then fifteen sit-ups also with 50 lb. weight, and fifteen two-arm pull-overs. Finally last exercise: arm curls, 50 lbs., ten with each arm.

My muscles have become hard as iron. This fills me with great unrest and strange desires. My shirt is completely unbuttoned. Words, ideas, plans, stock quotations feed into the endless ticker-tape of my mind. Life is streaming through me with breathless energy, sometimes a rush of ecstasy, sometimes a whirlwind of menace. I think the police are lurking in every sewer of society. I shout into darkness of boiler room. "Come out, come out wherever

---

*Editor's translation: "Darius and Parysatis had two sons, the elder Artaxerxes, and the younger Cyrus."

you are!" The kids stop playing and stare at me, puzzled expressions on their faces, but after a minute they brighten and go back to farting around. A fly starts to make a home in my ear. I light a cigarette. It tastes like a janitor's handkerchief. I throw it away. Acid sensations sweep down to my toes. Things are getting mixed up along the edge of my razor. I talk to the landlord's box: "No sir, not me man! I don't like to strap myself to a chair when I'm free-floating in the primordial vastness of my subconscious."

A strange region of my heart starts to unroll itself like toilet paper. I run my hand along the crack of my ass. A light breeze presses through the cellar. It might be caused by flipping the pages of a book. Suddenly fist at end of my left arm begins to quiver. A team of high jumpers is practicing inside my muscles. A rope is stretched between two points. A muscular young athlete leaps into space, body sideways, then stretched parallel he almost seems to be gliding, and as he rolls over the rope, he throws his legs up and kicks like a swimmer. In the next split-second his contorted face flashes by me on its way down. I notice that one of his front teeth is missing.

"Jesus Christ, it's the Olympics!" I yell out. "Sean, park your bike. . . . Hey Sam, but that basketball away. I want to go upstairs."

I'm holding the cheeks of my ass. Different parts of my body are moving independently. There's a wide valley with a railroad and small river running through my chest. My head fills up an empty space in the blue skies. The kids look at me as if I were a block away. They lower their eyes, stretch their legs, and say nothing. Going upstairs . . . halls smell of cabbage and frying grease . . . I tell kids story of a little girl, Nancy, who lived all alone in a village in the middle of the ocean, and how she and the house would disappear every time a ship passed by. A whale and a giant wave were her only friends, but they couldn't help her.

An exquisite story . . .

The kids scoot down the hall pushing each other to be first. Sam blurts out, "Hey Sean!" He's pissed off and starts to whine and cry because Sean pushed him against the wall. I guess the story scared them a little, but at the same time they deeply know that everything I say is a big joke....

The hallway is very long and ends at the gray dumbwaiter door. The walls are painted half white and half gray with a six-inch black line separating the two tones. As I stand there locking the cellar door I look around—the air moves very quietly but dumbwaiter door bangs open and disturbs the momentary peace. Something dark and criminal makes a flying leap through the up-and-down ropes of the shaft and dashes in slow motion down the hall and into my whole body. I burp politely and all hell breaks loose inside me. Two psychic forces of equal energy battle for the control of my senses. A curious duality is taking over my being. I see double, I think double, and I touch two locks. I am sure a new consciousness is taking shape deep down in the groaning library of my mind. My heart murmurs, my body shakes ... an indescribable state of nervous excitement. There's something inside me that desperately wants to get out. I feel it staring out wildly at the open dumbwaiter door and making leaps towards it as if drawn by some irresistible force. Every part of me has been wound up as tight as possible. My mouth drops open and almost instantly widens to fill up the hall right in front of me. I realize that I'm going to witness something supernatural, but I'm also scared shitless and a shudder of terror races through every nerve and muscle. A dark shape walks out of the enormous cavity of my mouth. Blissful weakness spreads across my stomach. Husky man about thirty-five with hands sunk in the sleeves of his black and white robe. He is a medieval monk, for some reason I think he's Greek. His eyes are dark, his stringy hair hangs over his ears, and there's a black spot on his chin, probably a patch hiding the ugly effects of venereal disease.... He doesn't move away. Now he is staring at me with acid eyes. He takes his right arm out of his frock, wipes mouth with back of his hand, then makes a cutting gesture with his fist across his chest. He speaks to me in perfect English:

"Once I lived in an impregnable castle. I had been given the knowledge of the Seven Powers of the World, I protected the magic mirror of life. In the keep of the castle there was a tree whose roots were the source of a stream that after several feet went into the ground. The mirror was in an open box that bridged the water. My own pride tempted me to gaze into it. I disobeyed the infinite wisdom of the Holy Ghost. All the things I saw were dusty and brown. I became a spirit thing and I have haunted certain people through the ages in the deranged senses of their visions. You are the first one to see me in the shadow form of my real self. To the others I have appeared as a giant chameleon. All of them tried to ask me questions about the many paths to knowledge and they were turned into flies on the end of my sticky tongue. But I don't know what will happen to you."

Africa's most notable animals suddenly show up and are smelling up the hallway behind the monk. A car starts to run amok. It's a convertible, pre-World War II model. Animals bang against the walls and pounce on each other. The noise is incredible. An ostrich, a lion, and most of the zebra disappear into a dozen eggs. The weirdo monk is eaten alive. I can make out a small path creeping through the blood and broken bones. The car's motor turns over. A cleanshaven, blackhaired man pops up behind the driver's seat. He combs back his hair with raking fingers. A dark cloud shaped like Australia is hanging over his head. The earth looks all purple and gray. The air smells wet and muddy like an empty fishtank.

I stare into the blinding front headlights. A tube of dazzling stars escapes right in front of my eyes. They lead me a long distance into myself. I am reconstructed in several seconds. I have eyes and hair but no nose. XYZ thoughts, a brain surge of dancing fire. Blood pulses into my neck. A floating, haphazard life. My visions become sullen, disconnected, cold, savage, and sick. My trembling hands are caught in a ferocious dream. Capsules of fear dissolve somewhere deep in the pit of my stomach. Showers of broken words collapse in my ears, and my body feels like a seashell.

—THE WORLD IS LOCKED INTO THE NEXT MOMENT—

Acid sensations sweep down into my toes. I shake my head in the wind. I try to jump. I go all the way up to the rim. Now I'm behind the car. At the end of the hall Sean and Sam are screaming at me to hurry up inside. Next to them, sitting in the dumbwaiter, a strong middleaged man calls to me with his fingers. His voice is as deep as a shoe. He has hairy arms, no nose, a serious beardframed face with lines on his forehead and tight curly hair. He's dressed like an ancient philosopher. Maybe he's my childhood image of God. Maybe He has three sisters.

I roll my eyes around searching for that safety path. There it is! Vague melting shapes. Get home quickly. God has called to me. I am one of the Chosen.

Acid sensations....

I race down the hall. My back feels a shooting gallery, a bull's eye between my shoulder blades.

Johanna is standing at the kitchen door. She touches my sleeve with her fingers—a graceful, beautiful figure in the bright sunlight of my eyes. She's wearing a light blouse and a dark blue skirt and holding her hair against the wind.

LANGUAGE AND MILD INCOHERENCE.

I explain to her my vision of life: "Johanna, a writer must recognize his superiority to lions, tigers, the stars, to everything in nature, even what's beyond understanding and appears to be miraculous, otherwise he's not a writer, he's just a sleepy wrestler or another crackpot cranking up a useless machine."

Johanna raises her eyebrows like windowshades. Her head tilts slightly. Three deep lines above the bridge of her nose. Thank God she has a nose. She takes my hands and rubs them gently. I hear a dog barking across the backyard. It's hanging out a kitchen window.

I think about what happened in the hallway. Was all that real? A stream of blood? Why didn't I kick that monk in the balls? Why didn't I jump in the car and drive it downtown? Why didn't I capture a giraffe? Is God still sitting in the dumbwaiter? Does he have a nose? Will I ever write a story that makes money? Should I keep trying to be a writer? Am I feeling sorry for myself?

My heart is pounding too much. My legs continue making loud noises. Sean is hanging on my arm and shaking it. Johanna tells him to "STOP!" He stops. Then he spreads his fingers far apart, opens and closes them four times, and tells me how much he weighs. Meanwhile Sam heads for the refrigerator and spreads his legs far apart. After three whole-body tugs he opens the refrigerator door. His baby arms are a couple of potatoes stuck together. He looks back at his mother and smiles mischievously. Then he sticks his melon head into every shelf searching for something he can enjoy right away. So I fix him up with a glass of chocolate milk, and tell him how great a baseball player his grandfather was. Sean has orange juice, and I drink my holiday special, vodka and apple cider, while Johanna pours bubblebath into tub and turns on the faucet.

Sean splashes water on my back, Sam throws it in my face. A black and white godzilla monster pinches my ass. Cobwebs fall out of my head. It's a crazy experience to take a bath with your kids and fifty thousand toys in a matchbox bathtub and I'm high on acid. Sensations all over my body. I feel as helpless as a magician's rabbit. Johanna magically washes all three of us. There's absolutely no room to do it yourself. She's sitting on the edge of the tub. She spreads a washcloth across my face, and after several minutes she takes it off. I see my face has been rubbed onto the cloth. This doesn't disturb me in the least. I plunge my wet wrinkled hand up Johanna's skirt and try to tickle her pussy. I tenderly massage the insides of her thighs. I am mesmerized spellbound by the melting sweetness and liquid darkness of her eyes. She squeezes my dick with a handful of bubbles. A rush of feelings, hallucinations!!! I'm higher than St. Patrick's Cathedral. I buzz over Fifth Avenue. Flags slap against my chest and legs. I'm falling . . . the swimming sensation of bliss. I close my eyes. I take off all of Johanna's clothes . . . slow, sensuous, and pleasant. We're naked. The strength of my body seems to whirl out of me and leap at Johanna in waves of visionary madness.

Johanna gently passes her hand through my wet hair. Brain

sweat. She tugs at my chest and stomach, then grabs my dick, the cat's meow! Acid is puffing up my head like a helium balloon. I hunt for shadows twenty feet away. My plus-minus fantasies are multiplying into imagination feathers and the taste of other events. Parts of me developing altogether differently in my mouth. My tongue explores inside of Johanna's mouth. Her eyes are closed. A blissful weakness runs down my legs. I feel sexy as an arab. My dick is pulled one way then another. Heavy breathing, heavy breathing. But Johanna pushes me away. "Johnny, no more now," she whispers. "Please, the kids."

The kids are playing monster face: Godzilla vs Frankenstein. They splash plenty of water on the tile floor as their eyes threaten all human accomplishments. Johanna takes them out of the tub, stands them on the toilet seat, and dries them off. Sam complains he's cold, so Johanna hugs him, and Sean sprinkles soapy water on his leg. I wonder if I should shave my beard off. I lean out of the tub and open slippery bathroom door halfway. A chill, a draft. "Hey Sean," I quickly yell. "I'll give you a dime if you shine my shoes fast." Sean's head pops through his undershirt. "And don't forget to put some newspaper down first."

I finish taking my bath without gorilla interference. I put on clean underwear, socks, dark brown corduroy pants, and yellow pale shirt with thin blue stripes. I bought the pants and shirt yesterday on 86th Street—also bought a jacket—after cashing my weekly paycheck. I work around the corner in a community basketball play-yard, but I never play ball on acid. It would box me out of my mind.

I trim my beard, cut my fingernails, brush my teeth, and comb my hair. I massage my arms and neck with an afterbath astringent. It smells like a hospital.

Out of the foggy bathroom! A change of temperature . . . acid sensations. A comb, a handkerchief, and six dollars in my pockets.

I gulp down more holiday drinks of vodka and apple cider. Almost ready to go. Sean presents me my shoes all finished. I present Sean with a dime. Johanna's smile is a good message. And meanwhile naked Sam runs in circles, pumping his arms, shouting: "One Mississippi, two Mississippi . . . four Mississippi, five Mississippi . . . seven Mississippi. . . ."

I am still laughing as I put on my new jacket, passion kiss Johanna—she's making coffee, she'll be up when I get home. I fantasize about making love—very vivid—as I head for the kitchen door. I'm off to poetry reading at St. Mark's Church. Sean's voice booms out: "Where you going, daddy?"

"Downtown, Sean. To a poetry reading."

Sean glances around the kitchen. "Can I go to the reading?"

"No, Sean. I'll be home too late."

"But not too late, I hope," Johanna quips and I smile senselessly.

Sam is listening. He's on the verge of tears. "I come with you, daddy!" he yells out. "I come with you!" I walk over to the kids, hug Sean goodbye, flick a piece of snot from Sam's chin, kiss him, then gallop out the door. . . .

The hallway was easy. No cars, animals, or monks. I step in front of polished mailboxes to size up my appearances. Can anyone tell that I'm totally freaked out of my mind? A childhood wild Indian run over by a car in the street. I rock my head back and forth to shake out sad memories.

I take out my comb. . . . A fly lands on it and crawls along the comb tooth by tooth. This rips me out of my mind. I'm ready to stab and kill. I see lines of acid around my eyes and wrinkles across my forehead. "Jesus Christ," I say out loud but to myself. "Ain't I a weird looking sonofabitch?" Out of the corner of my eye I see fly disappear. Instant Death! I hope Sean and Sam grow up tough, smart, and drugfree. It's better that way. They don't want to be like me because I'm a writer and drugs have squeezed my brains into a dry lemon. I'm already an Oddball of 20th Century Literature. That's a useful occupation. The Literary Footnotes of the Future need ME. Industrious scholars will investigate my teeth. They'll claim my face must have possessed that ecstatic look of a man startled out of the silent magic of a dream.

Yellow light scatters across my stretching fingertips. New visions are moving into 89th Street. I wonder if there are any bats in nyc. No . . . there can't be. I comb my damp messy hair, button up my jacket, and open newly-painted-black heavy front door. Acid sensations. Gust of east river wind hits me like a cold shower, but at least it isn't pouring out. I don't own a raincoat. My imagination is dripping with sweat. My ears move. My eyes listen. They are as fast as the speed of light. An overwhelming emotion! This need foaming at my mouth to search for everything in a night filled with bright noises, and sky above the buildings seems to be crumbling under heavy pressures.

Energy space agents from Earth leap high into overhanging stars. They're on the prowl for a sharper color-memory of flying dreams. . . . I might be on the dark side of the moon discovering lampshades. It doesn't matter because back in the warm kitchen Sam is crying his ass off. . . .

OPEN POSTCARD STORY

I woke up this afternoon at 3 o'clock and opened my front window. Cloudy out. Piles of sand and lumber. A stiff breeze. Kids carrying schoolbags yell, jump, and fight on their way home. A postcard lands on my windowsill. I examine it. On the front there's a black & white picture of a hand holding a roll of tape. On the back a stamp, an address, and the following message:

Dear Starlet.
    I miss you and I like to see you but the only way I can see you is by looking at the pictures that I have of you. Starlet I be coming home on a Monday.

P.S.
    I love you and miss you so much that I going to send you a suitcase of smack from here in Puerto Rico. Good stuff.

Love
    Donny

SLIP OF THE TONGUE

1. Black River

The stillness of philosophy is so primitive that a foot is startling disturbance. At least it seems so to a patch of tobacco or pole, whichever body is lighter. Even then it's more frightening than Black River boy hiding behind a thicket.

Vellun wets his fingertips. He's walking towards Black River. He doesn't make a sound, his feet are as noiseless as leather.

Vellun's a stone-cutter. He's familiar with soft buckskin boots, and movements or conditions echoing in black gulfs and disappearing behind soldiers. He's looking for his friend, Tonarm. There aren't many good signs for a stone-cutter in this part of Black River. He hasn't seen any children, doorknobs, rocks, or gold helmets.

He examines some tracks a few yards to his left. He's hungry. He hasn't found a brass chest, the only metal that glides easily into his muscles. In the North, which he remembers so well, laughter had made him open his eyes like a woman mopping sweat from trees.

He straightens up his head realizing that Black River boys had beaded his flesh. He was never very rich. He forgot distances at his waist from one boot to a short, heavy saddle. There were no mistakes behind crushed altars: he'd been drugged with a merchant's belt plain enough for a mule.

The thick stems of his fingers quiver. Something up ahead: darkening blue mist, or ears and lips forming a snake. It's Tonarm, not a snake. He has long hair. He's already divided the miles behind him into stories. He yells at Vellun:

"I was right! There are child-fiends . . . and gold dust . . . silk . . . and precious jewels. . . ."

He's told:

"Tonarm, your hair has turned blue!"

The forest might grow into a brass arm, but then centuries would have to be pulled together. When it's raining a piece of land will bend around a pack trail. Plenty of good times, instantly racing into deeper muscles, ache a little like water dumped into noise for fifteen years. Tonarm and Vellun lie down on the ground. They tell each other new stories. Their instincts are unconsciously holding the river like a snake.

Tonarm feels his hair stand up into different notes representing trails. An animal's crumpled body seems so close to revenge beyond medium height, but all interest disappears into numbers, which no one bothers to count on their fingers.

Vellun agrees with the additional table. He thinks that hunting on either bandage isn't dangerous on a natural ramp, but he can't glance back to a few pleasurable instances without altering bursting names. . . .

Once Tonarm and Vellun tried to colonize sponges. Their arms and faces were darkened by the sun as they puzzled through the riddles of older buildings and towers. Yellow forest crushed every border direction and indistinct warning. They didn't find any gold dust, but at least they'll never lose their eyesight. . . .

Edge of trail cuts into pair of saplings making one scabbard dive down like a cow. Proportions are destroyed, Black River boys are in revolt, or at war with each other. Time passes. . . .

Silkworms are everywhere, but Vellun is product of otter pelts. He doesn't really like farmhouses. He says:

"Tonarm, you're crazy. I don't like your new tricks. You've been crawling through that house for six months. All you found was a blue silk shirt. And what about me? I found a gold hinge, but I'm tired of living in this oak tree near two or three branches of Black River."

"We'll have to cross Black River," Tonarm says, turning around at last. "Some days I can just smell on my fingertips."

Vellun shakes his head as though he's been saving up dust for years. . . .

Some Black River boys had revolted. They wanted positions under rugs more than stamping their feet. The rebels, who were held together by the horn of a bull, had cut off their own fingers.

The real Fingers were almost invisible. This made them very powerful around Black River. They ruled in everyone's right hand so they wouldn't be noticed. They accurately measured small distances. Very few people knew they even existed. The Fingers could control thousands of Black River boys without them knowing it. Black River boys revolted by instinct every decade or so. Only once did they make giant attempt at revolution. A very long time ago they had been a prosperous and united tribe. All they did was fish or kill their neighbors until their fingers grew back.

This insurrection lasted for months. Ruins of the revolting villages outlined a pair of enormous hands breaking a horn. Only forty rebels were left. . . .

They have never heard of Tonarm and Vellun. Tonarm repeats his name followed by crude drawings of Black River boys falling out of green skies like hair. A meaning is growing, but it's still too scarce for this morning's large mouth.

Tonarm and Vellun join the rebels. Wheat is impatiently planted to expand leather so stars will halt at forest luxuries. Adventurers must regard themselves as fearsomely as silk instead of most inches. Frontiers are continued into outlines of a window and a door. Heavy bolts are needed.

Tonarm loves a good fight and hopes he'll be rich. He listens with interest to every kind of story, and likes to look at mountains, old buildings, towers, and ruins.

Vellun has formed himself into a hunger apparatus made from a new yellow drinking table and his restless teeth. He measures his legs to jump across strings, and then he eats freshly killed animal meat.

They both sit down in comfortable armchairs after dinner and stare at Black River. Tonarm says:

"Perhaps every new country jumps out of paper, then we could believe that there's a design in all my numerous stories. I want to be rich...."

Vellun leaps out of his chair. He's whispering:

"Tonarm, listen! I hear noises echoing over soft finger strokes."

He points into Black River. Tonarm doesn't get up. He says:

"Vellun, we'll have to fight our way across Black River."

Vellun puts his hands above his eyes.

"Won't we keep the ivory in working order suggesting heavy bolts?"

He listens to a very slow, careful answer.

"No! . . . You can't open a window when you don't understand who the Fingers are. They're wider than us, but only half our size."

Tonarm stands up and stretches out his arms. He remembers growing up under nails. But he can also step leisurely towards surprises, turning them aside either to wander back a dozen steps, or expect identical views to move in one circle like clouds around a tower.

2. Running Through Lips

Tonarm stands in the moonlight and washes his feet. Black River boys make him thirsty. Useless paintings spring up everywhere. He brushes aside candles arranged in overhanging trees and lips. He'll be the first to cross Black River. . . .

When he was young, Tonarm had been sold to the Fingers. They used children on wood floors and aprons to breathe heavier than chairs. He almost collided with copper statues.

Later he became a carpenter and a soldier. He ran away only to live near Black River boys. He was surprised that none of them knew about the Fingers. He built hiding places as they occurred to him. Black River boys told him monster stories about killer whose blood was in worms outside its skin. The worms crawled everywhere, especially in places where there were too many different languages.

Every two years Black River boys would paint some of their kids blue, and kill them. They built houses around the bodies, and threw their clothes on posts, which were hammered into the ground around the houses. They told Tonarm about flesh-craving child-fiends, who lived and farmed land near Black River, and who were very wealthy. Tonarm was interested in this wealth.

He looked all over for these child-fiends. He asked every soldier and merchant he'd meet about them. But he got nowhere. Sometimes he would wander along Black River drinking wine by himself, and hoping that Black River boys would build cities again and walk like men, who understand their own ugly shoulders and gaits. He would dream about fabulous wealth.

He trusted his own passions with a little belief somewhere outside his head that would lead him to balconies he could feel with his hair or gold dust in between the smallest grains of wood. . . .

Torchlights move in and out of the earth. Black River boys make tremendous efforts to open a window. Brown and green axes are forced into glass.

The rebel Black River boys depend on weaknesses that have gone through intervals or agriculture. They can't understand stories until they eat. They only see lines of dark men with snakes gathering around several thick poles.

Four rebel Black River boys run up to Tonarm and Vellun and

scream in one voice:

"We're not going to cross Black River. . . . Those posts out there are throwing up sparks as large as trees."

Tonarm walks away and searches for some vague blue lines.

"Don't worry, we're more intelligent than sparks because our skin has been clinging to shelves," says Vellun out loud, but a bit nervously. "We can draw lines faster than anyone else."

Vellun goes on telling them hunting stories. He also watches Tonarm crawling through soft threads which look like splinters. . . .

The merchants had never heard low rhythmical feet more than spreading fingers holding dim blue hats. Other buildings weakened the water supply. Vellun and his friends had been attacked by Black River boys.

Skilled woodsmen or stone-cutters often get caught in hiding places where a few white notches for letters can't be figured out in the same direction. Vellun hid in a leather belt supporting two walls on top of an open window.

He was lucky. Everyone else was killed. From far away Black River boys had appeared to be part of a valley. They couldn't jump across chairs. No one had taught them how to finish sentences.

Vellun couldn't get out. He became giddy and sick. He started to howl like a wild animal. His skin was stretched over a bowl of soup. He couldn't even move. He didn't think about his hunger as long as he could still recognize his own voice without trying to reach for a fork.

He was thinking about killing himself with a knife when he saw a dog sniffing at his teeth. The dog was a little bit bigger than Vellun. Tonarm stood beside it. He looked at Vellun and shook his head slightly as though he knew Vellun's thoughts. He helped Vellun out piece by piece. . . .

Four rebel Black River boys tear up trees around them and rush into the river. They die horribly. Eight more starve to death.

Naked children in doors and windows crumple boats together. Dimensions of the Fingers, who are covered with green hairs, increase a hundred feet below a room.

A few moments later Tonarm goes into the shallow water and closes a door. A wind blows in his face. All the remaining rebels are killed behind him. Their bodies form the outline of a man losing his hat.

Only Tonarm and Vellun are left. They run across Black River yelling like madmen. They scoop up drops of water with one hand so they won't fall off bridges. Vellun is wounded. Tonarm shoves long sticks and ropes through the lips, into the mouths, and down to the stomachs of hundred of Black River boys. Then his fingers touch empty meat barrels, and finally the beaks of soft birds.

They've crossed Black River safely. Tonarm shrugs his shoulders. There are splinters on the bottom of their feet. They take them out.

Then Vellun opens a door by himself, while Tonarm picks up pieces of glass and passes them through a loop. Doors, windows, and teeth fall into Black River like overcoats. They escape into the forest. . . .

The Fingers are very slow in getting up from the water, because they don't have any feet. They grunt like pigs.

The sun rises. Dust settles on crowds of Black River boys, who are standing or sitting in doorways, picking at their wounds. They don't remember a thing. Death has been forced down their throats as easily as a toothpick. . . .

3. Finger Paintings

Blue hairs suddenly grew in between the last sentences. Some were as wide as exclamations! Meanwhile every known source of sleep was giving great pleasure to Black River boys. They spent days in the air trying to mix new colors for their dead. They had used blue too often. . . .

Up until now the Fingers were like indestructible pipes connected to hinges and going from door to door. They secretly controlled most hands and fingers, eagles, sometimes barrels floating on water, snakes, and Black River boys. They especially liked to occupy distances stretching from the day before yesterday. For sixty years their hands rested on any small strength that might appear to be an illumination.

Instead of having ideals or beliefs they converted irrigation into dry sleeves every ten years. Now their bones have melted off. They tie their thoughts together into interesting moments and bury them in bundles of paper. Sound as absolute as sleep, complete control, and hate open up their heads. Then they can put words into their hands, and touch their wrists with any part of their bodies. . . .

The river banks curved back slightly into both forests. Black River cracks every fifteen years and returns to uninhabited battleground with water stains. That saved Tonarm and Vellun for the moment. . . .

Long ago Black River boys could easily defend copper, silver, and ivory. They build thick walls and nailed them between every tree. They didn't like to travel much. Then some Black River boys, who didn't have strong teeth, began to keep secrets in books. They pretended they could read, and they would smile all the time.

Art was established, and everyone rowed around the hills in painted boats. This brought on starvation, and sometimes Black River boys would look at each other like plums. They unconsciously painted pictures on broken wheels. No one saw these paintings except the Fingers.

Centuries of the Fingers had choked Black River. Threats riped into fruit and new thoughts were squeezed between doorknobs. Every wall was divided into slots faintly resembling leather. Dishes, a right or left hand, and large, round buildings were the new signs of wealth. Knots, loops, and wedges were also admired. Ceilings assumed an altitude of watches.

Once during a long drought Black River boys went crazy. Anything like movement of collars jumped into hand-to-hand fighting.

Everyone was burned up. Necks were broken, and long ugly arms were discovered a few feet away.

Black River boys began to whisper together when they covered their own flabby lips with buckskin boots. Chance fixed itself into their imagination like myth and then appeared on their shoulders. They started to look for someone else to kill besides each other. They threw rocks into the air and instinctively cut off their own fingers.

The Fingers hid under their many costumes. They examined, the dirt under each other's nails, and hurried noiselessly through tunnels and caves. They were really afraid. But they ended Black River boy revolution by bringing in the Crawler.

The Crawler was a large chunk of beef. Sometimes it was called the Frog-Gun because no one knew how it opened its mouth. Red and blue worms followed it around. It ate up every Black River boy in sight. It admired any silk shirt which suggested new diseases and foreheads.

At first the Fingers loved it, but then farmlands began to vanish. Food became scarce. Blue lines were growing in the river. Black River boys might all disappear. Decay slightly different in height boarded up every nail. The Crawler stayed in Black River for a long time, then it left without anyone noticing it.

Examinations crowded together very quickly and were absorbed into salt. Hunger was arranged on forks in the road, and the Fingers inspected all the food. Hunters, who were looking for new sources of meat, found lines of smooth stones leading into Black River. No one could figure out why these lines were there....

Tonarm has callouses on his hands. He's exhausted, but there aren't any oval shapes locked inside his head. He wants to keep running until he comes to a clearing in the forest. Then he'll clear his throat, and his teeth won't seem so ridiculous.

Vellun's hungry, he hasn't had any breakfast. His hand hurts. He's beginning to see things like chairs and buildings running in and out of his mouth. He doesn't say anything to Tonarm. He wants to stop and rest. . . .

Long hair isn't important to Black River boys anymore. They're slaves. Other arms have assumed startling bodies of water. They think they're going to fight a miniature army. Black River has been hammered into benches to avoid any precision. The Fingers have second thoughts, it might be a mistake, but they can change it later on.

Meanwhile they have other new buildings constructed. They pile all the lumber and nails behind worn-out couches. Black River boys are even allowed to paint. The Fingers want to have statues drifting between every room. The hallways will be circular. Numbers will be left on the edges, and the windows will be done in red leather. . . .

A few yards can puzzle the whole world. Comfort is one of the most important considerations. Music isn't necessary. There are too many ideas that can keep a man wide awake. He won't need sleep if his wounds are already open and cut into shirts.

In another minute Tonarm would've stopped breathing, but he sees this green chair. The road has evidently been dragged behind the chair. That's why it's rolling in a fit, so he has to follow it across his knees. He thinks all this might be helpful.

Vellun doesn't think so. All his theories have gone into his eardrums. He's like a madman who rushes towards a copper statue. He hates gold dust, but he likes freshly killed meat in very large containers. What if a giant attacked him? He couldn't do anything, there's dirt under his nails. He hopes he'll get back home alive, and then his skin will be decorated with stories.

He sits cross-legged in the comfortable green chair and dreams. . . .

4. Innumerable Legs

Respect makes friends nervous, but woodcraft is learned at night on ground equal to frames or wild borders. Then science will be returned to portraits, and music will unconsciously try to create color. Certain mixtures of blue will vanish through sound.

A break in wooded areas is followed by a pile of skins. Axes are recovered from some of them. An impulse through the soft ground doesn't quite make a carpet when icy mounds of hair shut out tendency for gates.

Moments later an eagle rushes straight towards innumerable legs. . . .

The Fingers were in every large mouth they thought was a window, while Black River boys explored a puzzle. Anecdotes had been pulled under doors and dropped alongside every hinge. These bonds were the last pieces of paper.

Black River boys leaped and danced as each door grew and expanded. They talked about everything under the sun except Tonarm and Vellun. Races were organized in every crack they could find. Nails were cut in half, and some Black River boys hammered their legs into huge birds.

Corridors led into deep, fertile valleys. Dense green and yellow fields stood at the end of long, empty halls. No one could remember their full strength. The Fingers swayed from side to side. They couldn't see. They were forced to stretch their hands over immense statues and long names. More than a dozen stomachs were lost.

Slow rhythms of fish bounced into thoughts of Black River boys. They had been born in one wide sleeve. Maybe that's why the Crawler thought they were so delicious.

The Fingers planted themselves underneath roads without touching up their paintings. They were afraid that night just might be another edge in a gray room. Then a hand waved in front of numerous legs after first words more than a feeling. . . .

In this part of the forest eyes are considered extinct. Animals remove their skins as if in bed. Chairs are more comfortable. Spaces are left within margins, but some of these are really windows. And every sound is open to leather boots.

Heavy copper nails have been hammered into the sky. Four stories extend to a blue roof. Tonarm has never seen such an animal tower. He slips into a chair and paints himself green, blue, and red. He sits there for a long time rubbing his forehead and chin.

"Vellun," he finally says, "it's been a suspicious half-century."

Vellun licks the palm of his right hand and examines the ground for gold dust.

Tonarm looks at the building's four stories. A thousand children are clapping their hands on the side of a mountain. Blue legs run across a desert away from green hills, a valley, and a river. A boy is eating a half-burnt piece of meat in front of burning house and fields. Naked boy and girl make love under an oak tree. Their soft clothes have been thrown next to a hinge and a red stick.

Tonarm turns his head away. The palms of his hands are sweating. He can't see everything at once. He lets go of some processions, which might make him shiver and run away. A blue silk shirt pops into his memory as though legs were tied over his shoulders.

Vellun stares at evening sun as he nervously rubs his stomach. He had butchered an animal, its tail is still flailing up and down. He didn't have to skin it. He has kept his arms in a wall and had hardly spoken to Tonarm since they crossed Black River. He thinks he's found a common name for strings tied around bronze or gold hinges. . . .

The importance of speed between intelligence and shaking hands was enormous. The Fingers had to spread out. They wanted to kill Tonarm and Vellun in the worst way.

First they banged legs into empty bellies. They stood up between tables and a wide room. Then they put on heavy bracelets. Tapestries were rolled into helmets. Shirts and belts rose safely above aimless leather. Any remaining traces of art among Black River boys were totally destroyed with all the benches. Now their bodies, especially their fingers, were limp and obedient. Their visions no longer jumped in and out of their lips.

Black River boys moved sideways through rustling leaves. They were expected to scan every line that went into Black River, and measure half the distance of each line into their throats. They found small fish bones and plums in the tall grass. They naturally lingered over the dark pits. They never worried about nighttime, but they were afraid that they might fall into a hole, so they walked around the floor a thousand times.

Now Black River boys were always naked. They knew that twenty mad dogs were inside a monster's belly. They wouldn't touch any of the silk shirts they found. They brushed aside some important frescoes instead of carrying hair through the openings. They thought that there wasn't enough room. Then statues sank into the mud. Carvings on trees and posts, which expanded from older stamps, started to confuse them.

Meanwhile the Fingers touched everything, They judged surfaces like a reflection: they wouldn't just sweep a floor, or talk to a dying man. They went inside things hoping to find surprises in a back room, which might have been a different color at one time. All this work didn't get them anywhere. They still hated Tonarm, but didn't have him. They wanted to cut up his present height and expressions with their own nails. Their obsession with breathless silence grew louder.

They decided to cross Black River. They made Black River boys do all the heavy work while they drew outlines around each new sentence and were absorbed in bandages like women. Then they fell noiselessly into entrances or over chains, which they thought were cobwebs, half natural strength and half division. . . .

A low blue sky like any other construction is really a box with lots of bright surfaces. There's no noise in architecture. Tonarm admires shining edges on old building, which he quickly climbs up to its blue roof. He feels he's taller than anyone else. He touches his feet and then he touches his throat. He notices new stretches of land. He smells freshly killed animal meat. He catches a piece of meat with his toes.

He thinks about drinking wine, or exploring each new sentence in his ears. He knows he had a certain number of sources, and he's beginning to understand indirect suggestions on dust and strings. He chews over his words. He would like to be rich and own thousands of blue silk shirts.

Moments of contact are scattered throughout his head. He wants to eat more or fall asleep. He tries to remember smallest grains of wood in the abandoned farmhouse. He passes his wind into the tower roof . . . an earthquake. He feels drops of water by his feet. He sees ninety-nine different views, all at once, of a brass chest, a nail, and the blue-tipped building. He tries to count Black River boys on his fingers. He can't. He spins around and around. . . .

5. The Crawler

The Crawler had been blue pygmy farmer near Black River a long, long time ago. He was the last of his race. He lived far away from the soft, gray roads of Black River boys, and a hundred feet below any reflecting surfaces. He didn't move around much. He stood on his head most of the day and watched moon rising every night. Sometimes he went hunting or else he'd sit by a pond, drink wine, and fish when he should've planted corn. He neglected most of his silk worms. He thought about lying under a bridge and jumping on whatever happened to pass by.

He liked to eat lots of things, especially snakes, chestnuts, sometimes a silk worm, and Black River boys, who were very hard to get. He would sing all day and rub the backs of his hands if he ate Black River boy.

He also liked to smell excited dogs until their screams grew louder. Snakes would quickly crawl up a tree when he put his head underground. But his only really bad habit was that he licked up a black ooze that came out of his knees.

He knew all the old roads and hiding places. This helped him when he was hunting food. One summer evening he trapped fifty Black River boys in a giant hunger spasm. He got them when they went into a cave, ate them all up in one meal.

Then his tongue became enormous. It grew longer each day with thick blue hairs every six feet. He couldn't smile anymore, sing, or even talk to himself. All he could say was:

"Slip of the tongue!"

The Crawler hated his tongue. It was red and slimy, and he couldn't cut it off. It replaced his head, shoulders, and chest. His lips had been first to go. They fell from a long line of paintings. His voice couldn't change the color of his eyes. Impressions of endless, faded rituals were formed into drops of water or silk worms. His tongue brushed against the highest branches on trees.

But he got used to it. He even began to think his tongue was very beautiful. The rest of his skin shriveled up, and many of his bones broke, but he didn't die. His tongue continued to be long, wide, and healthy. He could only wear silk shirts around his waist.

Years passed. . . .

He began to think he might be immortal, but alas, he couldn't see, hear, or smell. All he could do was taste, and he had to eat continually. He never forgot he was really a blue pygmy. He still liked to eat snakes, silk worms, and Black River boys, although he stopped liking chestnuts. He had acquired a taste for eyes and animal hair. One hundred and fifty years ago he was forced to cross Black River to satisfy these new cravings. He came back once and stayed a long time to eat up many Black River boys.

He didn't like the trip. At first he lost a lot of weight. The taste of Black River boys had changed, but he still hated them and wanted to eat them all up. He reduced his efforts so he could hide in Black River. He'd pass his wind into an earthquake. He was completely surrounded by pieces of string. Branches were meaningless to him like threads in his clothes. He even lost some of his silk shirts, the rest of them he tied into a knot and left under some leaves.

The Fingers loved him. They named him the Crawler, and sometimes called him the Frog-Gun. He hated this last name as much as he hated the Fingers. He wanted to eat them up, but he had a feeling that they weren't very tasty. He also thought that they captured Black River boys too quietly, they couldn't judge between trees and mistakes. He had to spend years in Black River washing his tongue....

Now his only other passion besides eating was carving images, figures, or stories on his tongue. It didn't hurt and although his arms weren't very long, his long tongue was very supple. It could bend every which way. Sometimes it would amaze him how well it moved.

First he carved images of shirts, pygmies, tongues, fish, and Black River boys. It didn't bother him that he couldn't see what he was doing. He knew he was doing it right. Once he had mastered everyday things he started to carve elaborate shrines connected to numerous tunnels deep inside his tongue. He loved pictures of silent, dusty rooms, or clusters of shaking leaves in a storm.

For the past fifty years the Crawler has been dying, slowly starving to death. After he came back from Black River, he didn't feel like hunting anymore. He still wanted to eat up Black River boys, and maybe the Fingers, but his small body couldn't support his tongue, which was like an old building. He buried himself in the ground, only his arms and tongue stood out. Flies and silk worms swarmed around him every minute.

He decided to paint the top of his tongue blue, and carve a story his father had told him from pygmy history on the front of it. The story was a very old one. Since no pygmy could write, their history and legends had to be passed down from father to son. The Crawler remembered his father walking with him to Black River. They stood in the water all day for two months until the Crawler had memorized the details of the story exactly.

Before the blue pygmies came to farm near Black River, they lived in the mountains. They were slaves of a stone-cutter tribe. Also they weren't pygmies: they were five foot eight, or five foot nine. The stone-cutters were very mean and warlike, and all over six feet. Other stone-cutter tribes weren't as tall. The ones who lived to the north of Black River didn't even build mountains. They were merchants and only built small hill ranges.

The blue slaves were forced to do heavy mountain work. They gathered rocks, cleaned them, and piled them together. All the stone-cutters did was cut the rocks and shape them into mountains. At one time they did all the work, but having slaves made them lazy.

The blue slaves worked in the morning and evening, and whenever it rained or snowed. The rainy season lasted five months. They weren't allowed to swim, plant corn, or wash themselves, but they could make babies any time they wanted to. Any slave woman who couldn't produce babies was thrown into a lake. Also the blue slaves weren't allowed to wear clothes, so many of them died from the cold.

Once a year they could meet together for a day of rest in a large mountain clearing: older men and women on one side, children on the other. Stone-cutters never guarded or interfered in any way with these meetings. Usually the children played with themselves until they fainted. The older people went fishing and drank wine in the morning. In the afternoon there was a big contest to see who could pass his wind the most times. Then they'd fight each other or make love until they fainted.

One year the oppression of the stone-cutters was worse than ever. It had rained a lot. Blue slaves were forced to build a whole mountain range. They even had to cut the rocks. And they were only allowed to pass water and wind every three days. Stone-cutters thought that this would make them work harder.

The blue slave meeting that year was different. The children were restrained. There was no desire to break anyone's legs in the dark. A man stood up and proposed an escape to fertile lands across the desert. The only objection was that the tribe was too big: if everyone tried to escape, they would move too slowly, provisions would be quickly exhausted, and then the stone-cutters could easily overtake them. So it was decided by the older people to let only children escape. The stone-cutters might not chase the children. Let the desert kill them, the lazy stone-cutters would say. It was also decided by the older people never to make babies again. The children applauded the decisions of their parents.

The children fled, but they were exhausted by the time they reached the middle of the desert. The stone-cutters were pursuing them with hungry dogs. The children didn't know what to do. So they prayed to God, Who loves everyone equally. He proposed a compromise: half of them could go on to the good farm land, of course with His help, but the other half had to go back to the stone-cutters. The children cut off their legs, and their legs ran around the desert until the stone-cutters and dogs caught them. God carried the children's better halves to the new land on a strong wind.

The dogs ate some of the blue legs, and the stone-cutters brought the rest back to their mountains. They ate the children's legs in front of the older blue slaves, who sat on the ground and masturbated in silence.

Meanwhile the children fashioned new legs for themselves, but they couldn't grow any taller. They became the tribe of blue pygmies. They settled in fertile valleys along Black River. They found many silk worms. Of course Black River boys immediately became their enemies. The blue pygmies postponed all marriages to fight for their new lands.

They defended themselves well enough with clubs and poison sticks, but they couldn't stop Black River boys from killing the silk worms and burning their fields and houses. Then Zogja, who was the founder of the Crawler's family, caught Black River boys burning his farm. He had just built a new house, cultivated more silk worms, and planted corn and an oak tree. Some Black River boys got away, the rest he killed. In a fit of mad blood lust Zogja ripped off a piece of Black River boy flesh and ate it.

He loved it. Nothing he had ever tasted tasted better. After that Black River boys carefully avoided his land when they raided blue pygmies. Zogja told all his friends how tasty Black River boys were. His friends agreed. Soon Black River boys never went near any blue pygmy farm. For a while pygmies even organized eating parties to invade Black River boy villages. They especially liked to eat legs.

Then the blue pygmies arranged their marriage settlements. Since there were two boys for every girl, fights were inevitable, but at least they were organized. Two farmers who owned adjacent property fought for a wife and each other's land.

The loser's body was hacked into seven pieces—nothing was eaten—and sewn by the woman onto a gold hinge, which was then nailed to the oak tree in front of the house. All new couples had to consummate their marriages under these sacred Hinge Trees to insure the prosperity and health of the future tribe.

But Zogja, after he had killed the other farmer, couldn't control his lust for flesh long enough to put the body and gold hinge on the oak tree. He made love too quickly, and also ate the dead farmer. He thereby destroyed all the hopes of power and greatness for the future blue pygmy tribe. . . .

6. Thousands of Splashing Blue Herons

Vellun is dead. One by one his fingers turn into yellow eggs. . . .

Vellun had always been fond of dogs, that's why Tonarm saved his life. Tonarm had been eager to look at mountains, towers, and old buildings, but he was also torn between his desires to caress silent animals and to cross Black River. Vellun thought all this was like an occasional story about wine or silk.

First they had been soldiers together, then they became merchants selling every ounce of milk they could get their hands on. They walked into houses more than a hundred feet wide. They sold doors and hinges very carelessly, and they listened to everyone's obscure story or legend.

Sometime Vellun felt bewildered looking into ditches where darkness was absolute. He'd see altars of gray stone surrounded by snakes and leaves. Once he found a weatherbeaten canoe. Boats really pleased him. He loved to sail for five or six hours on Black River. He thought he was very brave. He'd sit near the front of the boat and eat a meal without making much noise. At times like this his fingers didn't appear to be swords tucked under his belt.

But the proportions of their feet changed. They might have fallen off ledges. That's how Tonarm's dog died. Each line they found was divided into paintings so far ahead of their shoulders that even Tonarm couldn't recognize a small brass chest at any distance. To their surprise this was an astonishing relief.

They decided to do separate trading to gather more information. Tonarm crossed the desert, Vellun stayed near Black River.

He tried to bring his thoughts into a single current, but Tonarm had charged him with too many ideas. Unfortunately Vellun had a bad memory. He did very little trading. He didn't like Black River boys. They weren't as tough as they used to be—Tonarm had told him that—but he still wouldn't like to eat one of them. Maybe he thought about death too much. He searched for food every day. He was supposed to find gold dust, silk, and jewels, or at least make some kind of money. He didn't, although he found lots of silk worms. He also looked for flesh-craving, blood-mad, child-fiends. He really didn't believe in any such things.

He discovered many strings and a curious slime floating on Black River. He started to dig a wide tunnel under the river, but he gave it up because it was too difficult. One day while he was eating supper he found an abandoned farmhouse. He didn't look inside, but he left the door open. He continued to bite his tongue until Tonarm returned. He tried to remember his whole life four times. He noticed some red and blue spots on his arms after he picked up a rotten fishing pole.

Tonarm came back. Vellun met him near Black River. Tonarm had learned some amazing things, He told Vellun many new stories. Vellun thought that he exaggerated the importance of size, but Tonarm really could put himself into any crawling insect. He crawled into a tapeworm to prove it.

Vellun was afraid to look at Tonarm's teeth because they recreated the old home land of stone-cutters where he had climbed hundreds of times when he was a kid. He had moved into the North when he was ten years old.

Tonarm excitedly ran his fingers through his hair when Vellun told him about the abandoned farmhouse. He kept his head between his knees all the way to the farm so he could count the silk worms. Vellun thought it might rain. He still didn't believe in child-fiends. He watched Tonarm number and smell every worm.

They stayed six months at the farmhouse. They didn't find much. Vellun complained that his hands were shaking from hanging in a tree too long. He was dizzy and tired. He hated when Tonarm crawled between every grain of wood like a worm.

So they left. They crossed Black River. Vellun was wounded in his right hand while fighting off Black River boys. It was a small hole in his palm, but it felt like someone was trying to push a chair through it. They ran sixty miles before they stopped to rest. They poisoned every water hole along the way. He said nothing to Tonarm, but he really didn't want to explore for silk or gold dust anymore. . . .

Tonarm looks up from his dead friend. He isn't afraid of anything for the moment, but he doesn't know who killed Vellun, or why they didn't kill him. Maybe they couldn't see him on the roof of the old building. He might learn something by looking for knots in between his fingers instead of tying them up with strings, but he'd waste all his energy investigating every piece of wood or climbing up ropes. He might even become religious.

He gazes at the tower for a long time thinking about its pictures and cutting them up with imaginary strings. He pulls the strings. His throat is dry, and his tongue sticks to the roof of his mouth.

He hears himself say:

"There's no such a thing as a child-fiend. There's no lost treasure either. They're probably an extinct tribe of very short farmers, who cultivated silk worms, and who crossed Black River at one time or another. But this old building . . . might collapse."

He laughs out loud. Then he cuts a wide trail from the trees into a deep gulley, which surrounds the old building. He regretfully impales Vellun on a spear and leans him against the tower. There's a slight earthquake. He poisons the water in the gulley, and gathers up many dead branches and leaves. Then he looks for something under a rock....

Tonarm was in the middle of the desert. His attention had been attracted to an unusual point, which might have been missing from a chisel or file. He remembered vague stories that made his sturdy legs ache. He had wandered aimlessly from statue to statue.

He sat down near a large sand pile that was white with patches of blue in it. He watched a pack of senseless dogs, who had been following behind him for several hours. He wanted to relax. He was very thirsty. He mixed up stories in his head to pass the time. He dreamed he was swimming in Black River when his heart stopped. He thought his bones were sticking out. He tried to control his muscles at their greatest length. It worked because there were so many bends in this landscape. His body started to shake. He hadn't eaten in days. He caught a glimpse of snow-capped mountains up ahead when he bent over to untie his buckskin boots.

The pack of dogs led him to the stone-cutters. He saw them throwing their dead into a clear lake. They didn't seem too friendly. Tonarm calculated that their stones could touch every branch on a tree.

He introduced himself as a merchant who was interested in glass, leather, and stones. He remembered all the things Vellun had told him about rocks. He drifted past tons of theories. No one made much noise, but each sound was very distinct. Soon he knew everything by sight.

At first the stone-cutters didn't bother him much. He was surprised. They even taught him some interesting new tricks. They only hated objects, which were thicker than a rug, and which might remind them of the old days.

They had been drinking like toads for five hundred years. There weren't any more open spaces to build on except the desert. But their heads were wide open. After seriously struggling with a half dozen intricate systems—they also knew about hiding places—they could magnify rocks one jump after another. Then they gave it all up as nonsense. Now they can pass each other from mouth to mouth.

After a while Tonarm couldn't keep up with these crazy drinking stone-cutters. Vellun had warned him. Sometimes he'd just sit on a rock and get stoned all day. Like all other drunks the stone-cutters told him their sad stories. Once they had been very prosperous. They had owned slaves and built enormous blue mountain ranges. Vellun hadn't told him about the slaves.

Tonarm suddenly thought that every story he knew was put into numbers and gates. He decided to ask the stone-cutters about their slaves. He called them all together. But when he bent his head back to emphasize his story, they picked up stones and threw them at him. He had discovered all their sources.

He started to laugh. He knew that they couldn't walk straight in any direction, or for that matter even throw straight. They had devoted too much time to space. This had its effect on their feet.

He thought he had all the information he needed. He hoped he'd be rich soon. He started back towards Black River where he'd meet Vellun. Tonarm didn't know his hair had turned blue. The last thing he saw when he looked over his shoulder was a dim blue glow over the stone-cutter's lake. He imagined it was thousands of splashing blue herons coming out of the water. . . .

7. Blue Hair

Their wooly hair got caught in the river. They had been looking for fingerprints. Black River boys had decided that they didn't need to bring along their goats or sheep. They encouraged each other to walk on the water. Half of them sank before they reached the other side. . . .

The Fingers had once been very powerful. They had had the best hands in the whole world. No one challenged them as much as warning a shower. They had increased from a large egg like children hurrying to breakfast. They always sat down first, while everyone else stood behind them and bowed.

But they wanted to be invisible, so they gradually lost control over all other territories except Black River. Vellun, who had lived in the northern hills and traveled a lot, hadn't known about them. Tonarm didn't bother himself about them. He thought that their name had become a household name, but that was a very big exaggeration. They were still dangerous, and Black River boys, a warlike tribe, were their slaves. . . .

Black River boys started fires to keep warm. They were afraid. Their eyes hurt and they had sore throats. The Fingers rubbed each other nervously. Soon everyone was dried out.

Black River boys played with water snakes, and the Fingers naturally built copper monuments. Two giant severed hands, lying on a mat of long blue painted hair, spurted blood onto a door. Red nails fell into a corridor. On each side of this arrangement were two shining columns, which were as tall as trees. On top of each column a man sat in a burning armchair with a large rock in his lap. There was no doubt about the meaning of this monument: the Fingers felt very certain that they could kill two men twice over.

Some Black River boys discovered animal tracks and followed them. They slowly began to lose their voices. At first they had cursed their own noise, but then they silently ran back to the river leaving behind their weapons and best rugs.

The Fingers prepared for night marches. They were visibly altered inside heavy bolts. Some of them became very rigid, while others, who were extremely lazy and didn't care about Black River boys, thought hopefully about the Frog-Gun. . . .

The Crawler didn't know why these two men were here. He thought about stories of blue hills and mountains across the desert. He had been carefully trying to hold together his stomach, but like water which sinks into soft ground it had disappeared. He hadn't eaten anything in a very long time. There was some muddy water at the bottom of the gulley in front of him.

He knew Tonarm had blue hair. He could taste it. He wasn't sure whether they recognized who he was, but he could tell they weren't Black River boys or the Fingers.

He immediately liked Tonarm, who climbed all over him like on a building. Vellun's hands were shaking as he looked intently into the forest.

The Crawler remembered his father's voice. He stood very still and thought about the kinship and primitive outlines of colors. His father had often touched his skin in Black River. His father's fingers had been so sticky that some of the Crawler's skin had come off.

He was sure that Vellun was a stone-cutter. He didn't know how he knew, maybe he could taste it. Vellun impatiently walked around the gulley. All of a sudden he was anxious to discover a useful name, and then cut up old stones.

Tonarm fell asleep on top of the building. He tried to picture the abandoned farmhouse exactly, but he thought there was no reason why he should. The Crawler tasted copper in the air. He was restless. He had finished carving the pygmy history some twenty-five years ago. He strained himself to pass wind. He felt like he was going to collapse. He was slowly starving to death.

Vellun held a hunting knife in his open hand. He threw it up into the air and caught it. He thought he would like to spend the rest of his life eating good animal meat. He looked at every picture on the tower. Three drops of water fell on his head. He remembered gray altars and worms crawling out of broken nails. He was still afraid of the dark. His tongue hung out of his mouth. He could almost taste the spaces around him in a sudden flash of light. He was dead. He swallowed his own tongue. . . .

Black River boys were very thirsty. They had wandered around every tree for days. They had expected to find pools of water almost everywhere. But either the water had dried up or it had been poisoned. Leaves fell from branches of giant trees and floated in the air for hours. They always brushed against Black River boys before touching the ground.

Soft rocks were everywhere. They were probably caused by the intense heat. If Black River boy hit a rock with his axe, his axe would sink in half way and he wouldn't be able to pull it out. Huge soft boulders rolled or floated in front of them. Sometimes they would walk into a boulder and get stuck inside. Four or five skinny Black River boys walked through a boulder and out the other side.

Most Black River boys were going blind in this forest. Their eyes had started to fall out. Of course the Fingers could still feel their way in the dark. They touched piles of animal fur wherever they went. They also touched armchairs. They didn't care how many Black River boys died, there would certainly be enough left to kill two fugitive men.

They felt all over for a floor until they were almost covered with blue hair. Any point joined to a window or hidden from view was investigated. Tree roots were connected every few yards and posed like copper statues. . . .

The Crawler knows Tonarm is sitting next to his dead friend. Tonarm brushes some yellow dust off Vellun's cracking fingers. He looks around. The old building is cracking.

The Crawler is feeling great. He thought he didn't have any strength left. He had plenty, he was able to kill a stone-cutter. He dreams about delicious velvet-black bodies. He sways back and forth just a little bit. He isn't sure if Tonarm sees this. It doesn't really matter because he likes Tonarm's blue hair.

He tastes blood running up and down his tongue. Even the silk worms are restless. His arms move in the ground for the first time since he finished carving the pygmy history. He knows Tonarm is making a spear from a long tree branch. Tonarm impales his dead friend in front of the Crawler. The Crawler passes wind. Tonarm doesn't seem to notice. He puts his hand into the gulley water and then piles up dead leaves and branches everywhere. He looks under a rock until he finds a worm, which he puts in his pocket.

The Crawler tastes his own mad blood lust. He thinks of armchairs. His arms fall off. His spine starts to collapse. He feels that there are hundreds of delicious smells in the air. He's dying. Black River boys and the Fingers are resting in his chairs, which he put in the forest when he returned from Black River just in case he wanted to know if there were any animals nearby.

He tastes Tonarm's blue hair again. He wonders if his ancestor's parents had made any more babies. Tonarm puts himself into his pocket and inside the worm.

One or two Black River boys still have their sight. They see water in the gulley, then Vellun, and the old red and blue tower. They tell the others. Everyone runs past a worm to the gulley. Tonarm reappears, the worm is still in his pocket. He starts to light fires.

Black River boys slip on blood, which has poured into the gulley from the Crawler's tongue. Silk threads are weaved around their legs. Some fall asleep. The rest crawl all over each other.

Towers falling. . . .

"The Crawler! The Crawler!"

"Slip of the tongue. . . !"

Huge tongue slips into the gulley. Dead men walk in shadows of mad silence. No one can get out. The Fingers are crushed.

"Get the Frog-Gun. Croak! Croak!"

Black River boys are delicious, but the Fingers have little meat on them.

"Ah! Fried black meat. . . ."

A real blue pygmy likes to lick his chops and have a drink after dinner.

Poison water . . . the Crawler's tongue is burning. . . .

"Burp! Burp!"

Old building collapses. . . .

Tonarm watches belches of heat and flesh rise out of the gulley. He remembers smallest grains of wood in the abandoned farmhouse. He picks up some silk worms. He wants new silk shirts. Then he ties all his stories together and throws them into the fire. . . .

He wipes his lips with his tongue, and he goes back towards Black River. . . .

ABOUT THE AUTHOR

Johnny Stanton was born in 1943 in Manhattan, the son of Irish immigrants from Galway. He was an altar boy and Eagle Scout who attended Catholic schools and eventually graduated from Columbia University, where he fell in with many poets and writers of the New York School, including Kenneth Koch, Ted Berrigan, Ron Padgett, and Paul Auster. He published many of them, some for the first time, in his Siamese Banana Press, which started as a newspaper in 1972 and ended as a performance gang in 1978. He is the author of many short stories and the novel *Mangled Hands*, neglected by critics yet highly acclaimed by the readers who discover it. He has lived in the East Village for more than 30 years with his wife, the poet Elinor Nauen, a cat, and a lot of art.

ACKNOWLEDGMENTS

Thanks to the following for their generous financial support, which helped to defray some of this publication's production costs:

Hanna Bahedry, Thomas Young Barmore Jr,
Matthew Michael Barry, Sam Bertram, Brian R. Boisvert,
Ashley Bray, Lee Broadmore, Michael Broder,
Shannon Leigh Broughton-Smith, Jeffrey Canino,
Scott Chiddister, Danforth Clearmountain, Eric L. Collette,
J Coombs, Joshua Cooper, Parker & Malcolm Curtis,
Edward DeFranco, Craig Duckett, R Eggleton, Isaac Ehrlich,
E Gaustad, GMarkC, Jeff Goldsmith, Jason Gray,
David Greenberg, Adam Gregory, Everett Haagsma,
Aric Herzog, Tom Hochman, Dave Holets, J. Holmes,
Conor Hultman, William H Jewett Jr, Fred W Johnson,
Jacob H Joseph, Kiefer, Michael Klausman, Stefan Kruger,
Kyle, Mark Lamb, J. A. Lee, Nick Long, Will Lorenzo,
Tracie Lucas, Larry Luddecke, Elizabeth Lynch,
Joshua Magady, Donald McGowan, Jim McElroy,
Kelly McMahon, Jack Mearns, Sergio Méndez-Torres,
Kirby Miller, Jody Mock, Spencer F Montgomery,
Geoffrey Moses, Gregory Moses, Scott Murphy,

Johnny Stanton

Alexander Nirenberg, Michael O'Shaughnessy,
Devin Patterson, Andrew Pearson, Judith Redding,
Terry E Roberts, George Salis (www.TheCollidescope.com),
David W. Sanderson, Andrew Seal, Seda, K. Seifried, R Shinn,
Phil Skinn, Robert E. Slaven, Kelly Snyder, Yvonne Solomon,
Caitlin, Sean, and Meagan Stanton (love you Grand Daddy-O!),
David Starner, K. L. Stokes, Corey Stottlemyer,
Michelle and Perry Swenson, Patrick Tillery, Steve Tomasula,
Elisa Townshend, Tim Tucker, Sydney Umaña,
Alycia Vaillancourt, Chee Lup Wan, Elizabeth Weitzman,
Conrad Wendland, Christopher Wheeling, Isaiah Whisner,
Charles Wilkins, T.R. Wolfe, Pen Zeltser,
and The Zemenides Family

www.ingramcontent.com/pod-product-compliance
Ingram Content Group UK Ltd.
Pitfield, Milton Keynes, MK11 3LW, UK
UKHW040237250426
12048UKWH00040B/1552